AISLINN HUNTER

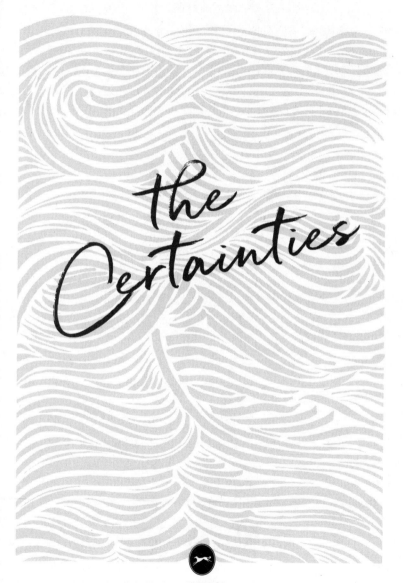

the Certainties

ALFRED A. KNOPF CANADA

PUBLISHED BY ALFRED A. KNOPF CANADA

Copyright © 2020 Aislinn Hunter

Published in 2020 by Alfred A. Knopf Canada, a division of Penguin Random House Canada Limited, Toronto. Distributed in Canada by Penguin Random House Canada Limited, Toronto.

www.penguinrandomhouse.ca

Knopf Canada and colophon are registered trademarks.

LIBRARY AND ARCHIVES CANADA CATALOGUING IN PUBLICATION

Title: The certainties / Aislinn Hunter.
Names: Hunter, Aislinn, 1969- author.
Identifiers: Canadiana (print) 20190152737 | Canadiana (ebook) 20190152745 | ISBN 9780735276871 (hardcover) | ISBN 9780735276888 (HTML)
Classification: LCC PS8565.U5766 C47 2020 | DDC C813/.6—dc23

Text design: Kelly Hill
Jacket design: Kelly Hill
Image credits: (waves) © CPD-Lab / iStock / Getty Images; (fox) © smartboy10 / DigitalVision Vectors / Getty Images; (binoculars) © Kreatiw / iStock / Getty Images; (glasses) © stdemi / DigitalVision Vectors / Getty Images

Printed and bound in Canada

2 4 6 8 9 7 5 3 1

Penguin
Random House
KNOPF CANADA

for Glenn, always

Narcissus.
My sorrow.
And the likeness of my sorrow.

—FEDERICO GARCÍA LORCA

Go now.
   Beside the uncertainties

in black veils
   stand the certainties.

—DERMOT HEALY

1 stand on my hotel balcony and look to the sea and to the sky's unbridled light. On the beach below, the gulls thrash and squawk; a vagrant scrounges for cigarette stubs. As I watch him, the same thought circles: when we are dead we will not know our nations.

The vagrant crouches in his baggy trousers, sweeps the pebbles with the side of his hand and pockets what he finds there. His hair is thin and patchy and he scratches at it frequently. For an hour I've watched him tread, barefoot, back and forth across the short stretch of beach. His feet have given me ample pause, as I've been up since dawn trying to decide if I'd prefer to die with my shoes on or off.

Sometime around seven the hotelkeeper dropped a breakfast tray outside my door. I can imagine the ants I saw on the ground floor of the hotel tipping their antennae toward the heel of bread and drizzle of oil. The old woman is long past apologizing for the weak tea or the size of the rations. Her sort is one we keep encountering: weary of us, of what trouble we might bring, even as she stuffs the crumpled pesetas we give her into a tin.

The breeze coming in off the sea is warm and fresh. Already, in the morning light, a man and a woman with skin still sun-kissed from summer wade out into the bay. She's wearing a bright yellow swimming costume, her dark hair tied in a plait. Beyond them a sailboat lolls gently in the harbour as if the world were not in tatters, as if this were simply another September day. Further out again, past the twin points of the headland, a merchant ship steams south, heading toward Barcelona, or perhaps as far as Tangiers. My death in front of me as I stand here: as palpable as that boat cutting through the water.

YESTERDAY AFTERNOON, before my companions and I were placed under detention, I walked along the Passeig de la Sardana to a restaurant called Paradou. There's a wine

I'm fond of, a hearty red by a Bordeaux vintner, and I was, if I'm being truthful, looking for something close enough to transport me back to better days in Paris. This wine was one I would drink with my friends from the philosophy department when we met at the café in Saint-Germain—the five of us under the café's striped awning arguing causality or perception as if we were closing in on problems that could be solved.

It was a quarter to one when I set out from the hotel, turning right onto the passeig. The street and the beach were quiet. A man in a clerk's uniform passed me without meeting my eye, and then a couple overtook me heading toward the pier. The old men occupying the shaded benches that faced the sea kept their eyes on the boats that had been pulled up above the tide line and did not turn to watch me. The buildings I passed under were weatherworn and pitted by bullets or gouged by bombs; there was a hole in the street which a woman casually walked around. Coming off the mountain the previous evening we'd passed by worse damage near the train station: the face of a church reduced to rubble; the remains of a house slumped between crumbling apartments.

Compared to the three Spanish restaurants I passed on my way to the Paradou—places with washed canopies and clean tablecloths, a few customers on their terraces—the Paradou was desolate. At La Dorada the tables lined up under the platane trees each had a vase of bright red peonies in their centre. How absurd, I thought: that people were still growing flowers; that flowers still willed themselves to

3

bloom. Unlike La Dorada, the Paradou's courtyard was gloomy and sour smelling. There were rivulets of water running down the cobblestones as if someone had sloshed a bucket at the source of the stench and then given up. There was no one outside, so I had my choice of the ten tables enclosed within its thin railing and chose the one closest to the beach so that the mineral lilt of the sea was before me.

While I waited for the server I watched a terrier pacing along the water. He was the kind of dog my sister had come to favour in her married life, and which, for no reason I could identify, I despised. Ritter was Meira's last dog, a chaser, bred for ratting, made into a pet, and killed in an accident beneath the wheel of a butcher's cart. I have always believed that if one wants to engage with an animal one must do so on the animal's terms, not demean him through an excess of coddling. Meira was the opposite, even had a special cushion for the dog, which she placed under the pearwood table in the drawing room. How her guests laughed at that the summer I stayed with Meira in Durbach.

Those dogs who seem closest to wolves are the ones who interest me the most. What breed was Salomé's pet? A wolfhound? Always slinking around the studio, and once baring her teeth at André when he blustered in drunkenly. I had been sitting on the chaise by the window and remember thinking, a bit too admiringly, that she'd tear André's throat right out of his neck if he weren't careful.

The table I chose had croissant flakes on it and a spot of jam. When the waiter did not arrive with a cloth I wiped the crumbs away with my hand and turned the table slightly to move the daub of jam to the side. It was nearing one o'clock and more people were moving along the passeig: a grape picker in his wide-brimmed hat, two men I took to be civil servants, a man in a railway worker's uniform who was likely heading home for his midday meal. None of them glanced at me though I sensed they were all well aware of my presence.

After a lull, a smartly dressed man in a black suit and homburg came along. Another marvel: that the market economy still flowed, that the man's suit showed little sign of wear even though production of goods was faltering and decent clothing had ceased to be affordable. This man gazed over at me—he had thick brows, a prominent nose and a soft chin that made him appear sympathetic. He nodded the slightest bit as he passed my table, and then proceeded up a stony pathway toward the hem of the mountain where three houses stood along a terraced ridge. The house closest to the passeig, the one the man entered, was yellow, and though it was dilapidated like so many of the other houses in the village, it had a kind of regal façade and what I imagined would be a magnificent view of the sea from its upper windows. To the side of the house, behind a low wall, a woman was pegging clothes onto a laundry line. In an attempt to quell my impatience over the absent waiter, I studied her efficiency and the graceful reach of her arms. As I watched her, the row of men's shirts and women's blouses grew.

Just when I was thinking I should get up and leave, a trio of hens appeared a little ways up the mount, clucking and squawking loudly and darting around a gate. These three hens were soon joined by two more who seemed to have escaped along a similar route. A flustered woman in a plain black dress followed soon after, reaching down to grab first one hen, then the other, with no success. She kept at them, though—rushing here and there trying to pluck them up or bustle them back into the yard. Such clucking frustration on the hens' part! Just when they'd discovered the larger world of Portbou.

One notices the strangest things in these years. How the woman chasing her hens—a middle-aged woman with a blue scarf tied around her neck—would, once, have been laughing. Laughter that would draw someone else, perhaps a neighbour or the absent waiter I was trying not to be pre-occupied with, to help: I imagined the waiter swishing his apron to move the hens along. The woman and the waiter would know each other, at any rate; there would likely be a measure of trust between them. But now, the woman looked frightened. Seeing her worried expression I entertained the idea of getting up to help her myself—but that would've been a joke. I'm fifty years old and my left leg is so stiff in the morning I have to set my jaw to the task of moving with any haste. This is not, as my travelling companions believe, the result of the strain of the journey—it's a simple hob-bling: age and exhaustion, a weak heart. My infirmity was the inspiration behind the insult delivered by my sister six months ago in my apartment in Paris when, frustrated by the futility of her attempt to coax me into going into exile, she'd shouted, 'You've already used up ninety percent of the energy normally afforded a life!' Meira had then stormed out of the room to keep me from seeing her tears.

At last, one by one, the hens submitted to the woman and cooperated; they were ushered, clucking, back into her courtyard, the curtain of her skirt pulled out behind them. In the midst of this quaint spectacle, the waiter, in the form of a shadow cast over the cobblestones, finally appeared. I shifted in my seat to better see him—his moustache thick and untrimmed; his eyes ringed black as if he hadn't slept in weeks. He asked in French what I might like. No menu—as if I came here daily.

'Un verre de vin rouge, Bordeaux de préférence s'il vous plaît.'

He nodded. A fly landed on his arm and he ignored it but I shifted my attention there, thinking of how flies are drawn to corpses, thinking that this man might already be, like me, so hollowed out by war as to seem dead to any living thing around him. 'Rien d'autre?' he asked, brushing the fly away and tugging at the cuffs of his shirt—a shirt, like mine, that had not been washed in days.

'Avez-vous de la salade niçoise au menu?'

The waiter bowed slightly and took a step back before turning toward the restaurant door. I smoothed my own moustache with a nonchalance I knew wasn't convincing. Even then, in those hours before Suzanne, Bernard and I presented ourselves at the station, I felt as if I were taking part in a play. The waiter and I were two grown men engaging in transactions as if nothing were happening: as if I were not a stateless man about to submit myself to the authorities, as if he didn't hold my well-being, my safety in his hands even then, capable of sending the dish boy to the policía if he were so inclined, to convey news of a foreigner.

Two days before we crossed the Pyrenees, we were told by Suzanne's contact on the French side that the Spanish authorities were allowing refugees to transit across the country. We were also told that the Abwehr, or some version of German intelligence, would be here in Portbou as well, both in uniform and out of it: at the train station and the port, and working with local informers to find refugees on German extradition lists. Suzanne's contact—a minor official in the mayor's office—had a copy of an extradition list from late August and our names weren't on it, but he cautioned us that émigrés were sometimes questioned and papers inspected closely enough that outdated documents or suspected forgeries were flagged. For these reasons it was best to appear to have arrived on a French train, which would mean that our papers would have been inspected in France. Our meeting with this man, in the back of a tabac near the station in Banyuls, lasted no more than ten minutes: he gave us the name of a local official and a hotel that he believed would be safe to stay in. He'd sourced three hats like those worn by the local grape pickers and said we should wear them coming down off the mountain and walk into town at dusk among the workers. 'No bags,' he'd said, eyeing my briefcase. No one was at the back of the shop with us save for an employee who looked like the contact's brother, yet the contact still nudged

the sack of hats under the table toward Suzanne's feet instead
of handing it to her directly. And so, as instructed, after our
long climb over the col we waited at the upper ridge above
one of the vineyards until the grape pickers started down into
the village at dusk, and Suzanne, Bernard and I walked in
behind them, exhausted beyond belief; my briefcase heavy
under the wing of my coat.

Going to the Paradou yesterday afternoon was a risk. If
Suzanne had known I'd left the hotel she would have been
furious. But I was tired of constraints and wanted to believe
that now that we were in Spain travel would be a question
of formalities—of doing as Suzanne's contact had suggested
and presenting ourselves at the station with the other refugees coming in on the four o'clock train from Perpignan.
We'd queue, get a stamp, and then take a later train south. I
told myself that if the waiter alerted someone to my presence—the police or the civil guard—I would still appear to
have the right papers. But no one exited the restaurant or
came down the passeig for me—only the waiter returned
with the wine in a cloudy glass, nodding as he set it down, full,
almost to the top. By the way his tired eyes met mine I understood that this excess was a gift from him to me and I
nodded up at him in thanks.

As I brought the glass of wine to my mouth my hand
shook, but then, when I had my first sip the visible world
slipped away. First, there was simply the taste: of earth and sun

and ripe fruit and easier, more carefree days . . . and then I remembered Hélène, my favourite waitress at the café in Saint-Germain, how she had the affectation of touching her earlobe when she spoke to us; the gap between her front teeth slight and charming even though it made her self-conscious. I felt as if I could remember everything about that life, that no detail had escaped me: the pigeons pacing the cobblestones with their cooing noises, pecking at the crumbs the breeze sifted from our tables, André cleaning his spectacles and frowning at Maurice's grand philosophies, Salomé's bell of a laugh, a paper napkin lifting up and then catching in a shrub across the street, Gaston stubbing out his cigarette and walking over to retrieve it and then waving that small white flag over his head as he came back to us.

It was only wine, *merely* wine as André would say, but in that glass I remembered that I had once felt full of the world, that my hunger was satiated by it daily.

After I finished my meal, the woman who had been pegging laundry on the house on the hill appeared again, opening her gate and coming down the path to the passeig. She was wearing a pleated dress that fell just below her knees and a straw hat over her boyish hair. Holding on to her gloved hand was a little girl in a mauve dress with a band of lace along the hem, and shiny black shoes bowed with ribbons. She looked to be about four or five years old. Like her mother, her dark hair was short. Neither of them shared the features of the locals, but in every other way—clothing and disposition—they seemed to belong.

Distracted by the absence of some item in her purse, the mother stopped just before the Paradou to rummage through her bag. The girl, loosened from her mother's grip, turned and walked toward me. It was maybe twenty paces to the Paradou's tables, not more, and then she was in front of me, her huge brown eyes staring inquisitively at what I cannot say—the empty plate and wineglass in front of me, or my face: my hair wilder than usual, my moustache in need of trimming, the skin below my eyes puffy and marked the slightest bit by the purple dye from my spectacles which became wet during the climb.

It occurred to me to say hello, to entertain her in some way, but that would have diminished what was passing between us in that moment: her world opening up, up, up and unfolding, and her taking me into that opening even as my own world was closing. A child saying, with the slightest lift of a smile, that it is all right, that the world will go on with purpose, that it may diminish but it will not end.

'Lo siento,' the mother said—and I blinked up at her fine, open face; noted her nervous smile. She had a small change purse in her hand now, presumably the lost object. I nodded as if to say that her daughter was not bothering me, and the woman, switching to English, said, 'She's a very busy child.'

'Je comprends,' I said. 'I understand.'

The woman smiled again and placed her hand on her daughter's head. If there was weariness in the gesture, an awareness of the dangers of associating with a refugee, she did not convey this—did not look down the street to see if she was being observed as the woman at the hotel had done, and as so many others had done in the weeks and months before this moment.

'I'm also a visitor here,' she said, taking her daughter's hand and leaning down to admonish the child with a whisper. 'Pia—' she began, and this was followed by a reprimand that carried within it the dual tones of chastisement and love. When her short speech was finished the woman reached across the table with her free hand and gripped mine quickly. 'I wish you luck, sir.' And then the two of them started down the passeig, the girl turning to wave goodbye.

I see you! her wave was saying.

And in my heart I said, *I see you back! I see you, I see you, I see you.*

I TOOK A DIFFERENT ROUTE to the hotel on my way back from the Paradou. I had been in Portbou less than a day and had otherwise not ventured out of the hotel, so it seemed silly to have a new route, but that was how I thought of it—a wilful detour from the expedient. It was a simple deviation: a left at the main passeig and suddenly I was on a secondary street and then in a square with a few humble shops and a market that consisted of a handful of carts arranged in a line, their sombre purveyors sitting behind on stools or benches—vendors who were far quieter than those I was accustomed to in the arrondissements of Paris or the streets of Berlin.

The man closest to me was selling olives. He was needle-thin and his legs appeared weak. Unlike the other vendors, who were sitting under their various canopies, he stood uncomfortably—one hand on the stack of crates behind him—as though his priority was to stand tall. Olives are a mark of luxury now. Though the market on Boulevard Raspail—with its baguettes, salamis and cheeses—was part of my everyday life before the war, such delicacies have long been relegated to the quarter of dreams. Even the niçoise I was served at lunch had arrived without its namesake olive, the tuna slopped in a mound over wilting greens, the dressing more oil than mustard, a few anchovies laced across the top where the olive should have been.

I had, I calculated, thirty pesetas in my possession; the rest of my money was hidden back at the hotel in various currencies, for bribes if necessary, and for the train to Lisbon and then a ship to America. The olives—a selection of six varieties in clay pots—looked bright and well procured though the pots were far too large for the meagre amount of stock. I was still full from lunch but I thought a small handful of something so fresh and vibrant might make Bernard and Suzanne happy.

In the pot closest to me were the manzanillas I like best: briny, firm, the slightest taste of almond. The vendor followed my gaze and offered me a sample, lifting an olive from the pot with a spoon and extending it toward me. I picked the olive up and smiled at him, revelling in the simplicity of the exchange. The manzanilla's flavour was delicate and just a little tart. The vendor had stewed it in a mix of lemon and young, grassy olive oil. In the pot to the left, filled with small purple olives, there was a quartered orange and an array of herbs. I hadn't seen anything like this in France in some time—a reminder that our war wasn't here, and that while the scars of their war were everywhere, the wave of relief I had felt crossing the border marker at the top of that intolerable mountain was not unfounded.

'Une louche,' I said, pointing to his ladle in case he didn't understand French. He nodded and, seeing I had not brought my own container, placed a scoop of strained manzanillas onto some newsprint, shakily weighing them on an antique scale. When he handed the olives over to me he caught my eye and glanced to his left, to the stand beside his—a fruit cart stacked with lemons, limes and oranges with a robust old woman in a grey dress sitting behind it. She was studying me, though when my eyes met hers she turned away.

I nodded at the olive vendor to indicate that I understood the warning—if that's indeed what it was—and handed over the amount owing. On impulse, I reached out and offered him a few extra coins; a small token that I hoped would appear to be part of the total. It wasn't much, but in that instant I could imagine this olive vendor's family—the shadowy presence of a wife and children—and somehow, in imaging them, in thinking about the war they had just come through, I felt more care for them than for myself. No words passed between us; there was just my hand under the dirty cuff of my shirt dropping a few final coins onto his rough palm. Without any hesitation, however—without looking up or down the street, and without a glance toward the woman I now thought of as an informant—the man stood as tall as he could, took the coins between his finger and thumb and handed them back to me.

As I turned toward the hotel, I saw a large painting hanging in a window in the corner of the square. I walked toward it. Above an unassuming doorway the words *Galeria Navarro* were lettered in gold. There was a sign on the door indicating that the gallery was open, a surprise under the circumstances. In France, all the galleries, large and small, were shuttered, and most art of value had been sent into cellars or the holds of ships.

The painting was of a landscape with a white horse in the middle of it. Not a horse with evidence of muscle and sinew as Géricault or Delacroix would have it, but rather the *expression* of a white horse: a ghostly figure with her head down to the grass, a grey whorl for an eye, standing against darkly outlined trees and a green register of field; the moon in the upper right-hand corner full and bright. In the bottom corner of the painting the date—1901—was inscribed sternly in red.

Inside, the gallery consisted of a single room with no furniture and no counters, just four white walls hung with a half-dozen works on either side of a curtained doorway which likely led to a storage area or private quarters. There was a long crack across the room's ceiling, and this crack, like the bomb blasts and bullet holes in the nearby buildings' fascia, and the rubble by the station, spoke to the fact that war had come to this place, too, dug its claws in.

The gallery's paintings were mostly landscapes, each an expression fattened by colour and line. The work spoke to me of that period of pastoral idealism in Germany at the turn of the century when a number of artists rejected the academy and set up a colony in the woods so that they could be in the world they painted. I stopped before each work, aware that this was a style that would be somewhat safe to display now—given that the men who might walk through the door could be corrupt Spanish officials, or legitimate buyers getting rich off post–civil war corruption, or German intelligence agents. I thought then that I should leave, that I was a trespasser, like someone who enters a bookstore only to discover that the books for sale are in a language the individual no longer speaks. I sensed, too, that my footsteps were giving me away: now I am walking, *step, step,* now I am stopping. But I was hungry for art, for how it makes me think, for its windows. And so I studied the work: a grey landscape with a marsh canal cutting through it; a stand of birch—and observed myself as if I were being observed, which led me to look toward the archway at the back of the gallery repeatedly until finally a man's balding head stuck out the slightest bit between two black curtains.

I nodded to him and moved on to the next work: a painting of a cowshed and of two cows pressing their heads between its bars, the far cow lowing and the near cow staring at the viewer with blind, empty eyes. It was by the same artist whose horse was in the window, the year marked again in red paint in the bottom right-hand corner. It was a work that broke with the pastoral because it referenced the torture to come. I was surprised at what it aroused in me . . . anger, frustration, a sense of doom. The cow's blank stare seemed not only a reflection of the ordeals we'd come through these past four months since leaving Paris, but also a study of the trap that is existence itself, the daily choices that all of us make, that are made on our behalf. It was, for me, as if that animal were not blind. It was as if what she, or he, saw was so awful the artist knew they could not render it in the work. A black slot: an animal caught in the prolepsis of the next moment's horrible dealings.

When I turned away from the paintings the attendant of the shop emerged fully from the back room. He was a man in a crisp shirt and brown suit wearing wire-rimmed spectacles similar to my own.

'Darf ich Ihnen behilflich sein?' he asked, bowing but hesitant. This presumption, his use of German, reminded me of my father who used to delight my sister and me with tales of the souks he'd visited during his years of study as an engineer. He said there was a trick, practised in almost every market in the Middle East, where the sellers, seeing a foreigner, would loudly proffer their wares in whatever language they thought matched the foreigner's appearance. The story of this guessing game entertained Meira and me to no end, and although in truth my father had often been mistaken for French or British before he was finally identified as German, he liked to embellish these stories—pretending the jewellery seller or the tea vendor had worked their way through twenty or more languages before finding one that fit.

'Monsieur?' the attendant tried to meet my eye. I smiled but said nothing. 'Oui, celui-ci,' he continued in French, referring to the painting of the cows and the shed but studying my face to see if I understood what he was saying. His French was halting but good. 'She is a German artist,' he said, 'one of the finest of this mode of expression. She died not long after this work was made.' He nodded his head again, a form of subservience that had probably served him well during the civil war, and backed away toward the curtain. I could have dissuaded him of any misperceptions then—that I was a customer, that I was a threat—but I was too exhausted. This turned out to be a good, if unintentional, ruse. For what refugee, with any sense, having entered the country illegally, would eat on a patio, enter an art gallery, and walk down the centre of the street in daylight in Portbou?

NOW, FROM THE BALCONY of this hotel, I watch the early morning swimmers. Their ease impresses me: how the woman in the yellow swimsuit and her husband, or lover, swim independently and then come together to talk, sometimes kissing on parting to swim out again, his strokes long and sure, hers of a shorter duration before she stops to wade in place. They watch each other more often than not: checking their relative positions and then making adjustments so they aren't swimming at too great a distance. The water must be cool now in September, still comfortable, though there would be a need to keep moving.

I've had five lovers. Six, if you count Leonie—though I was young and she was experimenting: teasing out a series of actions and reactions in order to understand her power. I was only twelve to her seventeen when she first kissed me. She was the oldest of my cousins and frequently left in charge of my younger sister and me during the one summer she came to stay with us at our house in the country. Kissing soon turned to other kinds of touching. She made it into a game, an ante of if-this-then-that . . . but I would have been happy either way: game or no game, overt manipulation or encounters of the more romantic kind. My parents had an excellent library in the country house, and I knew, from novels and clinical texts on anatomy, more than most boys my age. By August we were well on our way to having intercourse—Leonie having in her possession some sort of object that she said would prevent her from becoming pregnant—when my mother caught us with our clothes mussed in the tool shed at the back of the property. 'I've been calling for you everywhere!' she said, a look of fright on her wide face. And then her expression changed as if to say she knew the difference between child's play and what had, moments before, been occurring. Soon after, mother sent Leonie back to her parents, and although I felt the loss of her auburn hair and milk-white skin in a confused and sometimes tormented way—a way that I would come to understand involved both longing and shame—my concerns, in her absence, eventually returned to the more obdurate sorts of things I could discover through books.

That autumn, in what might have been a consolation prize for the loss of my cousin, I was given my uncle's microscope. My sister, Meira, was busy by then with her sports—with the temperamental horse my parents had bought her and with fencing and shooting and cross-country running. She was so fast at the latter that she'd earned a scholarship. Left to my own devices I immediately set out into the fields, collecting beetles and damselflies in jars, whereupon I would add a wad of wool daubed in ether to kill them. I would then make a grand study of their constituent parts under the microscope, complete with elaborate drawings and mathematical formulas to explain flight dynamics. My father, an engineer, called my hypotheses 'clever fabrications,' which he deemed evidence of a literary mind. Because of this slight and other, less overt, discouragements, I turned to the social sciences, though they had no such name then. I decided that I wanted to know how collectives worked and how group selection was made— how the hive of bees in the woods by the stream came to reside there and reside together, how the ewes chose their mates, how the lambs knew their mothers, why our bitch once killed her own pup. This was, perhaps, the greatest year of my childhood: it was a time when civic and national politics were not yet real to me, when the environments in which groups and individuals were raised and habituated abounded outside our estate windows and inside my classroom, and in our house: in the kitchens and servants' quarter downstairs where I was sent for cake, in the relations between my father and the groundskeeper, and at our own dinner table. This, I think, is when I learned to fall in love so easily—by watching others. Later, I realized this feeling of love, of heightened infatuation, was like my encounters with the work of Rembrandt: that effusive light that is both inside and outside the subject being painted. But back then, at twelve, thirteen, fourteen, it was something else—it was the bees bursting into a black cloud at some unseen signal, it was Meira's cat suckling her kittens in the barn, it was the power of seeing without being seen . . . it was as simple as hiding while Gerda stood at the butcher-block table working the dough off her fingers with such concentration, it was as if she were at prayer.

Yesterday when the three of us presented ourselves at the station, we did as Suzanne's contact had instructed—waiting inside the tunnel until the train from Perpignan arrived and then slipping into the station with the passengers who were disembarking. We acted as if we'd come in with everyone else: three more ragged travellers among a collective of fifty or sixty, lugging the last vestiges of our old lives in beat-up cases across the platform.

As we moved forward, four Spanish police officers appeared, checking papers and ushering passengers in one of two directions: Spaniards with identity cards were allowed to exit, while the rest of us were steered toward a large set of double doors that had been wedged open and led to a room that appeared to have once been a central waiting room or a customs hall. It had high ceilings, slow-spinning fans, and beige walls strutted with concrete pillars capped with Corinthian designs. There was a row of seats near the door to the platform, but most of the room was empty, save for the long tables where the guards were inspecting suitcases and the counter to their left where a clerk was stationed. Behind her, there was another room, or some-thing approximating a room—an area partitioned by a low wall—in which a half-dozen men sat at desks behind lamps and typewriters and telephones.

Suzanne waited in line with the other passengers to see the clerk, while Bernard and I stood near the door to the platform. The clerk was a local woman in the drab clothes of a civil servant, her expression stern, her dark hair wound into a tight coil at the nape of her neck. I wanted to sit on one of the wooden chairs lined up by the wall because my legs were still weak from the climb across the col, but the situation seemed to call for standing, so I remained beside

Bernard with a French newspaper tucked purposefully under my arm and my battered black briefcase wedged between my feet. The air in the room, just off the platform, was stale with cigarette smoke and the grease of the locomotives. I had to fight to keep from coughing. There were dozens of people in the queue before and behind Suzanne, mostly French it seemed, many likely trying to get to America on their papers, and a few German-looking like me. All of us were adults—as if everyone had sent their children to remote locations for safety months ago, as Suzanne had.

How many people like me, I wondered—stateless, stripped of their citizenship—had come through here? How many thousands or tens of thousands had stood in this room? I had, in my briefcase, identification papers, the appropriate visas, and six petitions for my care from French citizens of import. I had examples of my academic work and a letter of promise from an American publisher for my new essays on the *Metamorphoses*. Few others would have so much support. There had been a demand for my extradition in Paris, and the Gestapo had confiscated my apartment and what books and papers I'd left there, but I knew in my blood that the bureaucracy of the war was too great, and my significance too negligible, for any record of these transgressions to appear in an office such as this. Nonetheless, in the reality of the moment— the grey despondency of the people trudging forward, the clerk's unsympathetic expression as she questioned a woman wearing too light a dress for the changing season—I felt frightened. And standing there, my feet throbbing in my shoes, a procession of human bewilderment shuffling along in front of me, I tried to locate what I was seeing, what vision of the future haunted me. I looked to the woman nearest me—in her floral print dress and cloche hat and smart gloves—and her eyes were full of fear. The man in line behind her—his beard suffering from the lack of a barber—his eyes were also full of fear. I found myself asking of each—what have you done, what might they hold against you? I thought then of that line in Ovid's poem when Narcissus is at the pool studying his own reflection: 'He fell in love with an insubstantial hope.' What was our hope? That the disarray of the war neuter our interrogators? That we had now become as insignificant as we have been made to feel, so that we might slip through the cracks in our nothingness? Standing there in the shared misery of other travellers struggling forward with their papers clenched in their hands, I looked for myself . . . for some version of me . . . or for someone's eyes to meet mine with a look that said we would be all right. I realized what I was doing with a shock: at that moment, even after being on this earth for five decades, to still feel empathy most easily in those cases that reflect my own? This was a failing. Perhaps the greatest failing of all.

When Suzanne reached the front of the line, Bernard and I joined her. She smiled at the woman on the opposite side of the desk. 'Buenas tardes,' Suzanne said and then she gave the name of the capitán we'd been supplied with—Marco. The clerk raised her eyebrows at his name, swivelled on her stool and called out something I couldn't quite parse to the men stationed at their desks behind her. A few looks were exchanged between the officers—not of the sort that would occur when one is trying to locate a person, but expressions that asked, *Who will deal with this?* After a minute, a man in a pinstriped suit with a fresh haircut stood up, buttoning his jacket and stubbing out his cigarette in the ashtray on another man's desk as he came toward us. He was dark-haired and dark-skinned, as if he'd grown up on the coast. I immediately wished he was in a recognizable uniform.

'¿Esteu buscant en Marco?' he asked. He smoothed his moustache with his thumb and forefinger and looked Suzanne over coldly—her bright lipstick and smart brown dress indicative of Paris, as was her fair hair, her accent, her bearing. He glanced over at Bernard and me, who stood behind her, ragged as refugees, though we'd wiped our shoes, and scrubbed and dried our pant legs at the hotel so our means of entry would appear normal. 'Français? Allemand?' he continued.

Suzanne clicked open her purse and presented her papers, and Bernard and I handed ours forward as well. Then Suzanne began as rehearsed—professional, almost impatient. She introduced herself and said, 'Je parle au nom des ces personnes . . . I am speaking for these individuals . . . We three have transit visas for Spain and papers for America.' The officer inspected our documents and signalled that we should move aside with him, farther down the counter. When it seemed he was taking too long with our documents, Suzanne put on an air of irritation and asked for his name. He gave it—'Señor Porras'—without so much as lifting his eyes from our papers. Then he asked Bernard and me to step forward.

Bernard put both hands onto the lip of the counter to steady himself. He'd been ill since Marseilles and was weak from the climb over the mountain. From how he wavered beside me in his loose suit and cap, I suspected that he was running a fever again; his thinness, his gaunt face made him appear like some sort of mirage, not wholly present in the room. Señor Porras regarded Bernard for a minute and then turned to my papers and me. We had hoped to seem innocuous: people whose influence was limited to small academic or artistic circles, people whose work dealt more with esoteric ideas and less with political ideologies. This was, in truth, the case for Bernard: as a painter he's less of a revolutionary than most, though both he and Suzanne—whose husband is Bernard's agent—were part of an anti-fascist circle in Paris, and Bernard was one of six or seven artists I knew whose work the Gestapo had deemed degenerate.

What did I think of then, when Señor Porras was regarding me? Taking stock of my clothes, my face, and my expression? I thought of the briefcase between my feet. Of the manuscript on the *Metamorphoses* inside it and the notes from my last revision of the Narcissus essay—pages of new ideas dashed off in the Bibliothèque Nationale in the week before I left Paris—shoved into an envelope. I thought of my desire to have this manuscript arrive in safe hands and of the possibility that some German intelligence agent could find incriminating ideas in the work, ideas that weren't there—born solely from his own small-mindedness and his desire to see them.

We had hoped that our transit visas for Spain would be stamped without hesitation, that, at worst, the authorities would run our names against whatever new extradition list they had at the station and, not finding them, send us on our way. But more and more people were being pulled out of the line; more of the men from the back room were coming out to flip through visas and residency cards and passports. The counter to my right had become crowded, the man closest to me—twenty-something, German-looking, possibly Jewish—had a sheen of sweat on his face, and I wondered if I had the same.

'Monsieur?' Suzanne eventually asked.

Porras smiled and held up three of the papers we'd given him. 'I'm sorry, it's these transit visas. There's an issue with them now. All visas issued in Marseilles have been cancelled.'

'Depuis quand?' Suzanne asked. She looked toward the men who were still seated at their desks behind the partition as if she hoped that Marco, the man we'd asked for, might somehow be among them. 'We were told—'

'Yes, of course,' Señor Porras shrugged, 'if you'd arrived last week, two days ago . . .' He raised his open palms toward his shoulders. 'But there are new regulations effective yesterday.' He smiled again so that we could see the spades of his teeth. 'I'm afraid it's not for Spain to decide.'

'Might I speak with you in private?' Suzanne asked. He laughed, aware that she planned to try to bribe him. There was money stitched into the lining of her dress for this very reason.

'You can speak freely in front of my fellow citizens,' he said, waving toward the clerk and the officer beside him and the men in the back, clearly enjoying this show of integrity.

'May I see the man in charge of the station, then?' Again Suzanne assumed the impatience of a person with rights.

'He is not here today, either. Like Marco. I'm afraid I'm in charge at the moment.'

'When will he be in?'

'Tomorrow.' Porras lifted a silver case from his jacket pocket and tipped a cigarette out of it. 'Do you want to make an appointment with him?'

'Yes, I do.'

'Of course. I just need to know where you'll be staying. In the meantime, I will keep these.' Porras gathered our papers together and raised his eyebrows. Then he turned to the clerk behind him. He spoke to her quickly in Spanish and she turned and relayed his message to the men behind her, and one of the men in suits called out 'Alejandro!'

The German-looking man beside me was still standing at the counter in his nice waterproof coat. The officer he'd been dealing with was consulting now with another officer in the back room. I had to resist the urge to tell him to make excuses: he forgot his bag on the train, his wife was unwell, he must have dropped a paper . . . he was young and strong-looking and I thought he could move quickly, could get away in the confusion. But he knew, and I knew, that such subterfuge was likely to cause more difficulty than adhering to whatever new rules the Vichy government had put in place. Even for people like us.

Suzanne turned to me and Bernard and smiled reassuringly. Bernard, his head low like a dying animal's, scanned the room for the chair he needed. A minute later a young man in the grey-green uniform of the local cabos walked toward us.

'An escort,' Porras said. 'To ensure you don't take advantage of our hospitality.' He turned to the guard. 'Please ensure no one leaves the hotel. I believe they're staying at vídua Vivas.' He waved our documents in the air. 'Until tomorrow.'

We knew then that we had been watched, or that the old woman from the hotel had talked to someone. And knew that by the time we settled back into our rooms, our names would likely have been added to a deportation list—though it was also possible that our papers might be shown to German agents: passed over a café table or pushed across a desk on the off-chance that we might know someone or something worth trading our safe passage for. We knew this, and the man beside me knew this as he watched us walk away from the counter paperless and in the company of a guard. Strange, I know, but I was so grateful to have my briefcase. My identification papers? The letter from the Chair of Philosophy advocating for my value as an educator, attesting to my loyalty as a foreign national living in France? These meant less to me in that instant than Ovid's ideas about transformation and fate.

When we reached the hotel, the old widow who had taken us in opened the door. She saw the guard standing behind us and said nothing. She had a fan in her hand with some variety of pink bird painted in its folds. There was a quick exchange in the local dialect, the guard sheepish and the widow snappish as if they knew each other. The lobby smelled faintly of a bone or meat broth emanating from the nearby kitchen. We trudged up to our floor, the guard, Alejandro, waving us into our rooms, even though we wanted to stay together and talk. Some form of sustenance would be sent up around eight. And a time had been set for Suzanne to return to the station the next afternoon.

IN THE PAST HOUR more people have appeared on the beach, although the couple from earlier has gone. Now there are groups, not families: five men in swimming trunks who will probably transform back into Guardia Civil when they return to their uniforms; local women wading into the water in their modest costumes—citizens undertaking the daily regimen of a brisk morning swim in the midst of the continent's crises. In better days I might have felt a kind of affection for these women and men—the woman with the polka-dot kerchief whose peak of fabric is dancing over her black hair, the man who has the most boyish of the soldiers' bodies: concave chest, what looks to be a tuft of moustache above his thin lips. I might have loved them for some

perceived strength or fragility; some gesture. The young soldier, I note, is left-handed: he waves at someone on the
promenade, near the doorway of this very hotel. He seems
hopeful at first and then turns dejectedly back to the tidal
line, bends down to wash himself with a flag of surf.

I feel some discomfort watching this. I still have the habits
of an observer, but my heart is no longer in it. Behind me,
tucked in my pillow, are the morphine tablets I have travelled
across the border with. I will need at least ten of them and a
jug of water. I have only a teacup from breakfast. This means
that I will have to make several trips to the shared bathroom
with my cup or take the pills in that rank and dismal closet,
or preferably find some other vessel for water. I would like to
be in bed when I take the morphine. The thought of running
into Suzanne or Bernard in the hallway is unsettling. If they
knew what I was up to they'd try to stop me, or call a doctor,
or stay with me until the end even though I'd prefer to be
alone with my thoughts. Once Suzanne comes back from
today's appointment with Señor Porras's supervisor and the
bad news I sense is coming is confirmed, I'll find a way.
Perhaps I could say that I'm going up to pack my few things.
I could ask for a jug to wash with, I could ask the guard for a
half-hour to write some notes to my family and friends.
Already there is a note for Bernard in my briefcase, instructions on where to deliver my manuscript. A half-hour. If I
take enough morphine that will be all I'll need.

I'm not someone accustomed to leaving things un-
finished. I'd like the pages that I've spent the last years of my

life working on to be read. I'd like the questions I've scrawled in the margins to be answered . . . and I'd like to be transformed myself—from a man who did not understand his own thinking into a man who's catalogued some semblance of truth. This was Ovid's business as well—a catalogue of transformations in times of uncertainty, tales of those subject to the acts of capricious gods.

Of all Ovid's tales, 'Narcissus' fascinates me the most. There is, of course, the version we all know: Narcissus is in the woods, hunting. Tired and thirsty he stops at a clear spring to drink only to discover a figure in the watery mirror. He becomes spellbound by the figure's beauty—the twin stars of his eyes, his soft curls, the rosy flush of his complexion. He tries to clasp the figure reflected in the spring but his arms only meet water. And so he becomes transfixed: lowers his face to his beloved time and again, the beloved raising his face up to him in tandem, though they can never touch. In his longing he goes without food and sleep—he rages and sees himself rage, he weeps and his loved one weeps with him. Spellbound, he stays by the spring, his body wasting away until death covers him with its dark shroud.

What Ovid doesn't dwell on is the moment when Narcissus comes to know himself in the spring—or whether that moment happens at all. In some versions the boy thinks he is seeing another and dies of that longing . . . but there are versions where he comes to understand that the one he loves is himself. Yet what fascinates me is that even in those versions, this impasse is glossed over. What must it be like to look into your own eyes, to see every mote of your being: every room you stood in, every failure and feat, every slight and hesitation, to know your inconsequence and your magnificence in one breath? I imagine it must be like dying; I imagine it must be like death.

The air is strange this morning: the swimmers are not staying in the water as long as one would expect—as if the sea doesn't agree with them, as if a storm is coming. Down on the beach the men have now gone; the women towel their arms and necks. They're having a conversation in a circle, their expressions sincere. Ten minutes later they're off, carrying their bags and satchels, and I'm alone again.

It is odd to be thinking about this now, but it occurs to me that I've fallen in love hundreds of times. I've fallen in love with a street sweeper moving his arms as if he's conducting, with a fourteen-year-old soprano in Sainte-Chapelle singing Fauré's 'Au bord de l'eau,' with a prostitute leaning against a wall in Pigalle—her eyes closed as if no one can touch her. I have fallen in love again and again with my mother, whose arms encircled me during the questioning years of my youth, and Leonie, who opened her legs for me, and Artun, who gave me his notes to study when I veered off course in our last year of university to obsess over the social meaning of bridges. I have fallen in love with a pigeon whose wing was broken and who fought off the crow who tried to steal the bread I dropped for her near my customary bench in Arkonaplatz. I fell in love just yesterday, with the unconditionally curious expression on a five-year-old's face—with you, Pia—wide-eyed and happy, toddling down a passeig in uncertain times. And yet I can feel all that willingness to love the world ebb in me now.

This is what I know from paintings and books and from being alive at a time when the world is turning inside out, the present gutted like a farmyard animal: something must survive. Pia, I think it will be your mother and, in that future world, that cleft in time: you. I saw it in your mother's eyes. That fierceness. She will make and spin a web of life for herself and you will be reared in it. And you will be a survivor too.

Already I can see you on the island you will come to call home—as sure as I see my hand on this balcony railing, the scuffed toes of the shoes I've been debating since sunrise. It will be windy where you are, just as it's becoming windy here. You will have fallen asleep in a room with heavy curtains and a bedside clock insistent in its ticking. The sound of the wind will take up residence in your dreams, forcing you to shout across the distance between you and your mother, who is standing on the other side of a plaza in her good green dress.

It's your mother's dark eyes that I see in yours, and those same arched brows as if always questioning. Even as an adult, your hair will be short, boyish. There will be a scar on your left arm, a beige moon against your skin.

And so we are here, in your room on the island, in the world that is to come, waiting for daylight. Waiting for you to open your eyes and move through that stretch between sleep and wakefulness when it's easy to forget what country you live in, or if you are a child again or the grown-up you've become. My life ending as yours begins. The sky between us a wild and deepening blue.

*P*ia opens her eyes and gazes at the darkened ceiling. She can hear the wash of the sea against the rocks and the wind gusting. She pulls back her bedcovers, walks over to the window, and separates the curtains. On the patio below, a white canopy is being set up for this afternoon's wedding. It catches a current and snaps up in an arc against the grey sky, almost flying out over the edge of the cliff. The father of the bride pulls one end back down and shouts over the gusts to the best man, who is holding another corner and a coil of rope. From her window on the top floor of the hotel, Pia squints at the heavy clouds, then looks down over the chairs and tables—the hems of the tablecloths lifting in the wind. Even the ivied arbour is swaying. They'll have to move the wedding inside.

Pia's ritual since she arrived on the island six months ago is to stand at the window upon waking—to speak to the sea out of some small form of human deference. She now understands two kinds of water: the sea of the village where she grew up, with its sheltered bay and turquoise shallows, and this sprawling ocean with its mood swings. For days the water has been dark blue and lightly choppy. This morning the waves are deeper and slate-grey. Cano, her mother would've called it—grey like the hair of the old women in the village.

Last night, the dream again: Pia's mother standing in the plaza speaking to a man Pia does not know. And Pia, twelve, sitting by the fountain with its plinking noise and its beads of water like a chandelier whose diamonds are forever falling to the ground. Her mother in the dream is young and arrogant, is wearing her good green dress. Watching her, Pia knocks her heels against stone, waiting. It was a dream Pia recognized even as it unfolded because it's the dream she's had all of her adult life. At the end of it she'd woken up briefly—suddenly aware of how absolute the night was, of the wind battering the shutters.

PIA COMES BACK FROM HER RUN to a lobby full of people. The last of the wedding party have arrived on the morning ferry. On her way up to her room Pia stops on the landing and watches the new guests as they drop their suitcases and survey the lounge's ornate furniture and plush carpets; the ceramic vases stuffed with plump flowers. The bride, here since yesterday, flits around greeting everyone: two bridesmaids who look like sisters, the musicians her father hired, distant relations red-faced and queasy from their travels.

The bride's father fusses over his daughter—'How did you sleep?' 'Have you eaten?'—as if she were an egg that might easily crack. Then he turns to the bass player, who's setting his instrument case gently against the wall farthest away from the fire. 'Rough crossing?'

The musician nods, and the desk clerk, peering up from her ledger, says, 'You're lucky the morning ferry ran at all—the rest of today's sailings have been cancelled.'

Later, when Pia heads back through the lobby on her way to the kitchen, the groom walks into the hotel. A cry goes up about bad luck, how he mustn't see the bride before the wedding, and the bride ducks behind the front desk in a panic.

'What?' the groom asks, bewildered, as the father of the bride walks him back out the door.

The fact that there's a wedding at the hotel means nothing to Pia. She isn't interested in weddings, can't imagine getting married herself. The bride, coming out from behind the counter with an exaggerated expression of relief on her face, is in her mid-twenties, half Pia's age. Twenty-four, twenty-five—isn't that too young to make such a big decision? Then it occurs to Pia that she'd already lived in three countries by that age—and worked in five different kitchens.

The wedding is scheduled for four o'clock. At six there'll be fifty-two guests for dinner. Pia runs the day's prep through her head. The fish and veg will have already been delivered; the guinea fowl will come by truck at ten; and the chef will start at two, which means everything needs to be in order by then. The dinner is in five courses: local oysters on a bed of greens, a tomato and basil terrine, crusted cod and peas, guinea fowl with parsnips, and then cake—a three-tier monstrosity that's taking up too much room in the walk-in refrigerator. When Pia pushes through the double doors to the kitchen, the prep cook is already at his station dicing onions. He has dark circles under his eyes, his face is puffy and his hair is wild, as if he's just rolled out of bed. He asks Pia if the rest of the wedding party has arrived yet.

'On the first ferry.'

'You run today?'

Pia nods.

'How far?'

Instead of saying, *Past the village hall and the widow sitting in her window, past the field of brown grass that suedes the sea, and the sheep in their shagging coats, and the stone farmhouse, and the gusting headland* . . . Pia says, 'Ten, eleven kilometres?'

The prep cook grabs a fresh onion off the counter, starts to peel its skin. 'You're slacking,' he says.

THE ENTREMETIER AND PORTER come into the kitchen while Pia is checking off the deliveries. Sometimes the staff listens to the radio but today the reception is staticky so they work in silence. The entremetier is shucking oysters, hunching over the counter to do his knife work because he's so tall. Pia picks one of the shucked oysters from its bed of ice and places it in her mouth to test its quality. The entremetier studies her face. The oyster is good—typical of the island variety: a slightly brackish taste, the mantle firm on her tongue. She dips a spoon into the mignonette he's made, says, 'Watch the salt. These have more—' and here Pia's brain shutters over the word for salmuera. She closes her eyes, repeats salmuera, and sees herself as a child wobble a spoonful of mussel up to her mouth under her mother's sharp gaze.

'Brine,' she eventually says, and the edges of her mouth flick up in a smile.

When Pia was a child in the village by the sea, food was simple: the signature of the soil or a slant of sun on the ripe tomato was what gave a soup or a salad its bright acidity; the broth served with mussels was the flavour of the mussels themselves. Pia was ten when the family moved back to her mother's country, to the large city where her grandmother still lived. There, they ate a variety of mussels that were meatier and fuller than the ones Pia was used to, served with a broth of onion, parsley and hot pepper. For her it was as if a melody had been added to music she thought she knew.

Pia's grandmother—her abuela—was a fierce woman. 'Eat, eat, eat,' she would say, 'stop staring at your food.'

The old woman sometimes mimed eating as she said this, as if suspicious the girl's comprehension was poor. Then she'd give up and glare at Pia's mother, who could usually be found sitting on the kitchen counter smoking a cigarette or at the long oak table in the dining room reading the newspaper. 'So skinny,' Pia's abuela would say, 'she fusses over everything!' But Pia ate slowly only to stretch out the time, hoping her mother and her abuela would gossip: *Oh my neighbour, he this, he that . . . and so-and-so across the street is pregnant, and why don't you have another? And where are you going now for work, and when will you be back, and is it safe?*

Pia pulls a bucket of basil from the walk-in and takes it to the sink. If she closes her eyes she can remember the first time she tasted basil: in her abuela's city garden—two plants sprigging out of the earth beside unhappy-looking tomatoes. Pia is like a woman in a famine in this way: always thinking about food.

An hour before the chef is due, the prep cook and the entremetier fall into an argument about the fish. Pia walks over to them, inspects the prep cook's deboning. She turns over a slip of cod. 'He's right,' she says to the prep cook, 'try not to make such a mess of it.' There's silence for a minute and then the porter—a local boy with a wide face and curly hair—turns the radio back on. Static. Outside it starts to rain, grey fingers tapping the window above the sink.

THE RAIN COMES DOWN IN EARNEST, and the location of the wedding ceremony is moved from the hotel patio to the village hall. Hotel staff help shuttle the chairs and tables down the road to the hall, a former schoolhouse. When Pia heads to the bar for a coffee she passes the father of the bride, his coat soaking wet, talking to the hotel clerk: 'Can we get some extra candles for the tables? It's so dark in there.'

The bar has filled up for lunch and the room is noisy with chatter. Pia slips past a group of local women waiting for a table—one wears a perfume that's a burst of violets—and asks the barman for her coffee. While she waits she watches steaming plates of food coming out of the bar's small kitchen—roast and gravy, a hearty stew—and checks to see if people are enjoying what they're eating. At the front of the bar, by the quarrelled windows, the musicians are setting up their instruments. After dinner, the wedding party will go back to the village hall to dance, and there'll be live music here for those who prefer to stay at the inn.

The lunch guests are a mix of locals and wedding party members. The man Pia sometimes sleeps with—a builder who recently moved back from the mainland—is sitting with a friend at a table along the wall. He has his back to Pia, which means she can choose whether or not to go over and say hello. She tries to remember how they'd left things: the builder in her bed as she got up for a morning run . . . and then nothing for weeks.

Pia puts her hand on the builder's arm. He blinks up at her. His face—its cragginess, how tired he looks—always surprises her because in bed his body seems so youthful. He's wearing a thick brown sweater, nubby under her fingers, and she remembers he still doesn't have heat in the cottage he's renovating.

'Do you know Pia?' the builder asks his friend, and the friend and Pia nod at each other. She's been on the island long enough to know most of the locals. The builder wipes his hands with his napkin and then sets it on his plate. 'Can you sit?'

'No, I have to get back.'

His eyes sweep over her face, inquiring. 'I was on the mainland,' he says. 'Sorry I didn't let you know I was going, something came up.'

'It's fine,' Pia says, and means it.

Pia first met the builder on a morning run. It was late spring, the island lifting its face toward summer. After the coast road turns inland there's an unfenced flock of sheep, and then a cottage. One morning there was a man outside the cottage, resetting rocks that had fallen off the stone wall. He waved, and Pia waved back. After a few days of waving, he happened to be working along the front of the property. He stepped out on the road to ask how her run was going. At first, Pia didn't say anything because when she ran she tended not to think in English and his words were like steps that lead you out of a dream. 'I hear you're the new sous-chef, working over at the hotel,' he persisted. He scratched the side of his nose with his thumb—a Roman nose, which at some point had been broken. Down the road a group of sheep moved slowly toward them.

For a long time, Pia and the builder didn't exchange names. Over the next few weeks he'd shout, 'Hey chef,' and she'd call, 'Hey builder,' and in the hours and days between sightings she never thought of him at all.

BY TWO, WHEN THE CHEF ARRIVES, the wind is buffeting the building. He comes in with his dark hair wild about his head, his face wet with rain. Pia hands him a clean towel. He pats his face with it before handing it back so she can walk it over to the hamper.

There's a sound the wind makes that's particular to the hotel—because of its position on the promontory above the sea, its flat stonework. Pia feels like she can hear the wind circling the building, whipping its head around corners to course along the stone, drag its knuckles along the windows. There was no wind like this in her childhood—no stretch of patio with frazzled grass, and no thin wire fence against a sudden drop to the ocean.

'Bad out there?' Pia asks.

The chef buttons up his white jacket. 'They called all the boats in a few hours ago.' He turns to the porter. 'One of the boats from the south harbour hasn't come in yet. It's not your father's—he's in, but I thought you should know.'

The porter nods and goes back to the saucepans he was scrubbing, peering up at the square of grey sky framed in the window above the sink.

Once the chef has made sure everything's in order—the quail plucked and cleaned, the sauces started—he tells Pia that the widow's son is one of the crew on the boat that's missing. He knows that Pia or the hotel owner sometimes will take the widow a plate of food to make sure she's getting enough to eat. Last night Pia had set aside an onion tart from the dinner menu for this very purpose.

'Why don't you stop over now, take her some soup?'

'Does she know? About the boat?'

The chef shrugs. 'Probably not, and it's too soon to upset her. They're still trying to call the crew up on the radio.'

The widow is in her eighties. Sometimes she will offer Pia tea and then come back into the living room carrying a vase or a colander instead of a teapot. A few weeks ago, after Pia had warmed up a meat pie, the widow asked Pia to call her husband in for dinner. There is a photo of him on the mantel: a gentle-looking man in his fifties with a strong nose and a mischievous smile. A man stuck in time, in a suit and tie from the decade he last lived in. Pia had brought the photo in and gently placed it next to the widow's small pour of wine.

On this part of the island there are almost no trees. It's possible to walk out a door and be blown over by a wind you couldn't see from your window. Pia learned early that the ribbon of road along the coast could alternate between stillness and sudden gusts. One morning, when she was out running, the wind had been so bad she'd been forced to turn around before the chapel and walk slowly back to the hotel, keeping to the inland side of the road. This was when Pia met the widow. She'd reached the windbreak of the village, and the widow—who lived four houses down from the hotel—stood up from her wingback chair facing the picture window to wave Pia inside.

'I keep seeing you . . .' the widow said, wavering in the doorway in a long grey cardigan, her hair white and thin.

She reached out to touch Pia's face and Pia, surprising herself, let the woman run her fingers lightly over her hairline. 'I half wondered if you were a dream.'

Pia knocks on the door and the widow answers. 'Come in, come in,' she says. Pia's wearing the prep cook's thick oilskin coat but has given up on her umbrella in the wind. Once inside Pia stands dripping on the entry rug. The widow disappears and Pia hears noise in the bathroom— cabinets and drawers being opened and shut—until eventually she comes back with a hand towel.

The first time Pia was invited to the widow's house, she noticed a peculiar scent she couldn't quite place. There were the expected smells—of black tea and dusty shelves, the must of the sea breathing through stone; a trace of the talc the widow had probably dabbed on that morning. But under all that was something chemical, like wallpaper paste or adhesive. The smell turned out to be binder's glue, which the widow used for book repairs. In her forties, fifties and sixties, the widow had been the island's self-appointed librarian. Her husband, a carpenter, had fitted out the back room of their house with floor-to-ceiling bookcases and, over the years, the widow built up a good collection of books. Five days a week she would take a selection of these books on a blue bus—also outfitted with shelves—to various parts of the island: the south and north ports, the main town by the lake, the fishing village on the peninsula.

Now there are at least a thousand books in the widow's back room, call numbers inked on each spine. In the corner of the room there's a wicker cat bed, its cushions lit with strands of white fur, although in all of her visits Pia has yet to lay eyes on its occupant.

Over the past months, the widow has lent Pia a number of books. Sometimes Pia will ask for books on certain topics—food or cooking, recipe collections—but also natural histories, novels about distant cities to remind her that she doesn't yet know where she'll end up.

'How's your Roman history coming?'

Pia looks up from her cup of tea into the widow's bright blue eyes. Some days, the old woman's mind is remarkably sharp. 'I'm only at the Punic wars.'

The widow smiles. 'Well, there's a lot more bloodshed to come.'

On three or four occasions, in the widow's back room, Pia has played a game. It was a game she and one of her girlfriends used to play in school: both girls would close their eyes and let their fingers trail over the bumps of the spines of books in the library. When either one of them called stop, they'd open their eyes and slide out the books their fingers had landed on. They had a pact: no matter what the book was, they had to read it. Pia had played a version of this game in the widow's back room, and the book on Roman history had been one of these selections.

The widow finishes her soup and bread. She talks about the charity raffle at the church, about the problems with her milk delivery, how sometimes the bottles are outside the door at six and sometimes at seven, and she isn't sure if it's because of the new delivery boy . . . and then she says, 'I still like to get up early,' and peers across the sitting room as if she can see a scene from some other time in her life playing across the curtains.

When Pia stands up to leave, the widow says, 'Thank you for coming.' Then she adds, softly, 'He'll be all right.'

Pia swoons with relief. The widow knows about her son's boat.

IT'S JUST PAST SIX P.M. WHEN the wedding party crowds into the dining room. Midway through the meal Pia stands at the kitchen door and looks out its round window, like someone below decks peering out the porthole of a ship. The room is light and airy—the best man laughing at something the groom has said, the guests regarding the food on their plates thoughtfully even as they chat across the tables. Dinner is the chef's hour. After the last course he likes to walk around the tables in his crisp jacket, greeting the locals he knows, shaking hands with the men and bowing to the women, his dark hair falling forward as he kisses their hands. Pia has imagined this role for herself: how she would navigate the room, what degree of attention, of affection, she might be able to give.

Tonight when the chef comes back from the dining room, he looks pleased. The prep cook's shoulders relax, the porter steps out for a cigarette, but Pia scrubs the range harder, working off the splatters of sauce. She thinks: If I sit down on the side of the road midway through a run no one notices, but here, in this space, the chef sees everything. And her contract is almost up. The island has so few tourists in the winter and the restaurant isn't busy enough to require a full staff. Pia hasn't yet decided where she wants to land—if she should pack the small bag she came with, leave with a good reference, or ask to stay and see what else she can learn here.

'Great work,' the chef says. He pats Pia's back and then rubs his own eyes with the heels of his palms. 'Finish the clean-down, then you can head over to the dance if you want.'

All the staff from the hotel are invited to the dance. The hall, a one-room building with wood floors and a peaked roof, is the usual spot for local festivities. Pia sprints to it through the rain with the prep cook. She's wearing her only dress—blue silk, short-sleeved—one that's too light for autumn. By the time she and the prep cook duck inside the main doors they're both soaked. The bride's parents have made everything beautiful: the hall's rafters strung with white bunting, the ledges of the stone walls lined with tea lights, lanterns hanging over the dance floor. Dahlias are bunched in vases on either end of a table stacked with brightly wrapped gifts. Soon, the father of the bride gives a toast to the happy couple and someone puts a record on— bright, up-tempo music—and everyone begins dancing. In the gaps between songs Pia hears the rain pummel the roof.

At the makeshift bar at the back of the hall, Pia finds the builder. He's wearing a collared shirt and dress pants, shiny black shoes that remind her of the ones her father would wear to business meetings. 'Red or white?' he asks.

Sometimes, when she drinks wine, Pia thinks she can taste the country it came from. Tonight, her glass of red is earth and ripe fruit with a hint of green grass. It reminds her of the village where she grew up—the grape pickers coming at dusk off the terraced hills. She glances at the builder, sees that he looks preoccupied. When she asks what's going on, he tells Pia that he had to go to the mainland to help with his daughters, that his ex-wife has decided to move back to the island so she doesn't have to manage things alone. Then he adds that the fishing boat from the south harbour still hasn't come in. The last radio contact was hours ago. He turns toward the front of the hall and takes a swig of his drink, his brow furrowed.

A song Pia doesn't recognize comes on and a cheer erupts amongst the wedding party. Pia and the builder move toward the front of the hall to watch the bride spinning circles under the lanterns, her satin skirt billowing and the lantern's squares of light falling all around her, and around Pia, too—across her arms, the moon of her scar, her hands.

Suddenly Pia is by the fountain in the plaza again, looking over at the man her mother is speaking to. He's wearing the dark trousers and light blue shirt of a middle-class man, his sleeves rolled up, sunglasses peeking out of his shirt pocket. She sees him as she always does, even as another part of her is searching for a detail she's overlooked all these years: the man waving her mother over, and her mother sitting Pia down by the cascading water—*Stay here.* Then the man and her mother move away—and when they are almost the size of cutout dolls, the man grabs her mother by the arm. Her mother leaves the plaza with this man, heading toward a row of parked cars. She doesn't look back at Pia, not even once.

This is her mother's first disappearance.

BY NINE O'CLOCK the rain is coming down so hard that the roof of the village hall starts to leak. The crowd thins, and those who stay dance around buckets. At ten the barman says, 'They're worried about the roads.' The groom's family, who live on the north end of the island, gather their coats and head toward the door. They don't want to be stranded if the road washes out. Everyone else makes for the hotel— the groomsmen holding jackets over bridesmaids' heads. At the hotel, the groom lifts the bride, mud lacing the hem of her gown, over the threshold.

In the bar, the quartet is playing up-tempo jazz—a tune Pia can almost remember. She thinks of a club she and one of her girlfriends would go to—in the basement of a run-down building in one of the poorer parts of her abuela's city. There was no sign above the door, the windows were always closed . . . but every night there was music and everyone, even locals at the end of long days of labour, danced until four in the morning.

The barman tops up Pia's glass of wine, ignoring the builder. This is because there's a rule about leaving the island and coming back, some sort of penance to be paid that Pia has yet to understand. As well, the builder had married a local and moved her to the mainland, and it seems that many of the islanders hadn't forgiven him for the failure of his marriage, or for leaving his wife and daughters in the large house they'd bought in the city and coming back here alone.

One morning, shortly after she and the builder started sleeping together, Pia had bumped into his ex-wife. This was outside the builder's cottage as Pia was on her way for a morning run.

'So you're the cook?' the ex-wife asked. She had a large box in her arms, and she held it carefully as if whatever was inside was breakable. 'I just think you should know,' she said, and this was followed by a long string of *he this,* and *he that* . . . the box weighing in her arms as the two of them stood in the early light, the girls in a nearby car with the windows up, staring forward. His ex finally saying 'you know, when there are children involved,' and Pia saying nothing because their worlds were, at that moment, so far apart—these notions of possession, of ownership, want. 'If he'd stayed in medicine things would've been different . . .' She'd said this and then stopped talking, seeing a flicker of surprise cross Pia's face. 'He's a doctor. Didn't he tell you? Left a year after his clinical training.'

The builder leans against the bar talking to one of the local fishermen. In the weeks since he and Pia were last together, he's had a haircut, and the flints of grey at his temples stand out. When he senses Pia's gaze, he reaches out and places his hand on her back, his palm warm through the fabric of her dress. The builder isn't aware that Pia knows he was a doctor. *It's none of my business,* she'd thought. Though once or twice, when he was touching her body, she wondered about it. Did he think as much about the workings under her skin as he did about the feel of her skin beneath his fingertips? The builder takes a long drink from his glass and sets it back down on the bar. 'Shall we?' he asks. And because she can see in his face how easy it is to fall into something out of laziness or habit she thinks *no, not yet . . .* and she closes her eyes and lets the quartet's brassy sound become a hot afternoon on a busy street in her home country as she tries to find a spot of shade.

The widow's son walks into the bar just before last call. He has a red welt on his cheek that will be a bruise by morning. He drapes his arms over the oak counter in a show of exhaustion and orders a drink. 'I'm famished,' he says. 'Don't suppose there's some leftovers in the kitchen?' A handful of islanders gather around him, and he tells them that he's come right off the boat, though—of course—he did check in on his mother, let her know he was okay.

The barman drops a pint of beer in front of him. The widow's son takes a long swig, then continues. The trawler ran into trouble in the swells just as they were turning back to port. They lost one engine, and then the radio went out. 'Then we saw a flare. Way off in the distance. We went after it for maybe an hour but had to turn back.'

One of the kitchen staff sets a fish pie down in front of the man, and he picks up his fork, holds it over the pie for a few seconds as if he's forgotten how to eat. Then he looks the barman steadily in the eyes and says, 'Honestly? I've been at it, what? Fifteen years? That sea was the worst I've seen.'

The bar starts to empty just before midnight. One of the locals who'd left earlier returns in a heavy slicker to say that the road south has started to flood and might only be passable for another half-hour. The bride and groom, who'd been holding court at a back table, make a round of the room. They say good night to everyone before heading tip-sily up to their suite. The quartet keeps playing, and the barman pours Pia a last glass of wine.

Pia rests in the lazy feeling she has now: of having done a good day's work, of being unwound by the wine, of the ease of having the builder beside her with his hand on her thigh. Sometimes it surprises her that she can feel so good and grounded yet still be comfortable with the idea of being transitory. In two months' time she could be anywhere in the world—in a city she's never been to, in a kitchen she can't imagine, in bed with someone she can't conjure at all. For a second Pia thinks, smugly, that it's because she's will-ing to run toward things, that what she's been through has made her brave. But then she thinks of her mother—of the last time she saw her—and as the quartet finishes its set and the last of the hotel guests applaud, her confidence in her bravery wanes.

When Pia was ten, her mother told her that every feel-ing you ever have lives on inside you long after you feel it. Like cracks in your bones. She said this as they stood on the street outside of Pia's new school in the city. A boy had shoved Pia for trying to play with his football, and she'd fallen, scraping herself on the paving stones. Pia held her arm up while her mother inspected the injury. A teacher had wiped it clean hours before, and Pia remembers wishing there had been more of a mark—a larger gash, fresh blood—something beyond the red welt and small cut she presented to her mother as proof.

'All of this feeling,' her mother had said, drawing a circle around Pia with her finger, 'all these feelings, they stay. So choose how you want to feel . . . Are you sad or are you angry?' She was using her professional voice—the one Pia knew from the radio. Pia studied her mother's expression to see which would be better: sad or angry. After a minute her mother grew impatient. 'Tell me the boy's name,' she said. At ten, Pia hadn't understood that she had a choice, that she could handle this herself, swallow it down. Or, she could give over her power. And so she had told her mother the boy's name.

Pia never knew what, if any, repercussions occurred because of this. It was as if a curtain had been drawn, and she was protected from the dealings on the far side of it. But, too, it was as if she had exiled herself—made herself super-fluous, precious, in a way she knew her mother disliked. And the boy? He never spoke to Pia again. And so Pia studied his careful avoidance, that distant orbit he maintained when the bell clanged and children were let loose into the sunlit schoolyard. This was an orbit she learned to replicate with friends and lovers—and it served her well every time she told herself to pick up and start over again.

THE BUILDER BEGINS TO UNDRESS as he enters Pia's room. It's the smallest room in the hotel—under the peaked roof on the uppermost floor, the ceiling slanting from its highest point just left of the entry to its lowest point above her bed. Some nights the builder forgets where he is, and he sits up in the dark and smacks his head, saying '*Ouff.*' The walls are lilac and the windows are hung with heavy curtains that block the morning light. Right now, though, the windows are dark and pummelled by rain, a rhythm Pia finds soothing.

Pia watches the builder's reflection in the wardrobe mirror, his fingers undoing his shirt buttons. His hands interest her: how careful their movements are, how clean he keeps them—for someone who spends so much time with hammers, nails, stone and wood.

Pia thinks about the things doctors see that most of us don't. When she looks at the builder's hands pushing his trousers down to his ankles, she wonders why he hasn't told her more about himself. Pia doesn't know much about the medical world. Her abuela was a woman of concoctions—grey pastes for burns and milky teas for colds or chest infections, a cure-all bitter soup that tasted of nettle. But once, when Pia was fourteen, her mother was hospitalized. The call came suddenly and so Pia's abuela took Pia to the hospital rather than leave her alone in the house. Everything there was white and brightly lit and people were either moving very quickly or as if through brume. Pia and her abuela entered the room a nurse had indicated. Pia's mother was sitting up in bed with her hair brushed down around her shoulders, bruises on her wrists, her eyes dark as river stones.

'What?' the builder asks.

Pia realizes she's been staring at him, at his hands. And because he asks, she tells him: 'I'm just thinking about your life as a doctor.'

He steps out his trousers, stands there. 'Who told you? Not that it matters.'

'Your ex, the day I ran into her outside your cottage.'

She feels the moment between them like a knife—a knife held above an animal bone you're about to sever, over flesh you're about to slice.

The builder says nothing, as if he's weighing what to say. Then he gives up, and moves toward Pia. And she thinks: *the body is also a way of saying*. Just as he cups her chin in his hand, bends down to her, the lamps in her room flicker: once, twice, before fully going out.

Pia hears the builder thump his knee in the dark. 'Do you have candles?' he asks.

'In the top drawer of the dresser.'

The builder rummages around in the drawer. After a minute he strikes a match and uses the flare to locate a candle and light the wick. He finds a second candle, lights that, drips some wax into a glass seashell intended for a guest's jewellery, and then he presses the two candles into that waxy base. He pulls his trousers on, opens the door to the hallway, and sticks his head out. All the lights in the hotel are off.

By the time Pia and the builder get dressed and wander downstairs, some of the guests have already gathered. The night clerk has set tea lights from the dining room along the mantel in the lounge, and arranged some candles on the round wood table. The bride and groom are on the sofa, groggy with sleep, the bride bundled up in a blanket. The bass player and pianist sit in the wingback chairs and one of the groomsmen perches on the stone ledge, poking a coal fire to get it going again. The room and everyone in it are dun-lit—like the seventeenth-century paintings Pia once saw in a museum.

'What time is it?' Pia asks.

'Just past two,' the night clerk says. She apologizes as if she is somehow to blame, saying that storms are a common occurrence on this part of the island but the generator usually kicks in. When she stops with her reassurances, there is silence and Pia is suddenly aware of the wind: how hard it batters the building and how loud, so that it's almost impossible to hear the rain.

THE BARMAN, WHO SOMETIMES stays overnight on a bunk in the office, and the builder gather up some tools and put on slickers and head out to the back patio to take a look at the generator. Pia picks up a candle and heads to the kitchen. There are a few things in the refrigerator that won't last without power and she's the only one from the hotel restaurant staff with room and board. She takes ice from the freezer and lays it over the fish, the eggs and the dairy—because people will still want breakfast. Then she stands in the kitchen trying to think of what else she needs to do, listening to the wind rattling the windowpane above the sink.

Pia is holding her candle up to the pantry when a draught of air blows out the flame. In the dark the smell of garlic, onions and root vegetables flares alongside a tang of smoke that must come from one of the cured meats. And suddenly Pia is in two places at once: standing in the middle of this kitchen in a storm on the island; and in the house in the village by the sea, a six-year-old whose mother wakes her in darkness, saying 'Vamos, nena'—pulling her arm so hard that Pia is yanked out of bed. Then she and her mother race down the stairs and through the dining room and kitchen. Before Pia can even ask what's happening she is thrust into the closet where the house's former inhabitants had kept potatoes and onions, and where Pia's mother now stores coats and shoes and her husband's rifle. Her mother closes the door, whispers, 'Por favor, por favor, cállate,' and cocks the rifle.

In the silence of that closet, Pia leans against her mother. She listens to the noises in the house: men entering, their unfamiliar voices, footsteps. She reaches down and picks up one of her father's shoes. And when the footsteps come closer, and the voices of men casually talking pass by the hiding place, she tries not to cry and so sucks on the toe of the shoe. Outside, the sideboard or the china cabinet is knocked over: a *thump* and a crash of glass. 'Una bonica foto,' one of the men says, and then some flying object hits the wall and the voices are laughing again. Pia stays perfectly still, wishing her father home from business, wishing herself still asleep in her bed. She thinks then about the asp her father once showed her in the grassy foothills above the village, and how she was afraid and wanted him to kill it, but how he said, *No, we'll leave it, this snake is only sleeping.*

The generator kicks in and illuminates the kitchen at half-lustre: the clean prep station, the glistening appliances. Pia takes a deep breath, then picks through the pantry for something to offer the guests. She returns to the lounge to find a dozen people gathered around the low table—sitting on the floor, sprawled on the sofa and the overstuffed chairs. In the muted light of the sitting room she can hardly see the guests' faces, but their hushed conversations are calm. The bride is nestled under the crook of her husband's arm; the pianist sits sideways on the wingback with his long legs dangling over its padded upholstery. Pia lays out some bread, cheese and fruit, then goes to the bar and comes back with two bottles of wine. The hotel owner is on the mainland, but she knows he would approve—a wedding night, the windows rattling.

The talk, as the guests eat and drink, is easy. Everyone has a story about an encounter with the natural world that has affected their sense of safety: a river flooding its banks, an ice storm, a small earthquake in a foreign city where the groom and his friend held onto a lamppost while the city shimmered.

Hearing the groom's story makes Pia think about one of the recordings she has of her mother's radio broadcasts. In it, she is covering a major earthquake. Her mother's voice, in English, dispatched to an audience halfway around the world: 'The houses are gone . . . the roof of the school has collapsed . . .' Thanks to the recordings her abuela made, Pia has maybe two or three hours of her mother's voice from those years. There are also other recordings Pia found amongst what was left after her mother was killed, including one made from a safe house where her mother was meeting a group of workers and students organizing a strike, her voice on the tape saying, 'We are moving inside now but it's too dark to see . . .'

The conversations around the table have become quieter and more private—people speaking to those closest to them. The bride has fallen asleep on the sofa and the groom, still awake, gently strokes her hair. The groomsman laughs at something the trumpet player says, his face lit with pleasure. The builder, the barman and the hotel clerk have been in the back office for some time now. Through the open door Pia can hear the chatter on the shortwave radio, reports of a distress call.

Pia brings more tea lights in from the restaurant, and opens a third bottle of wine. The barman had come in a while ago to switch off some lights, saying it was unclear how long the storm would last and that they needed to conserve the back-up generator's fuel. But none of the guests in the lounge—the musicians, the bridesmaid with the rope of auburn hair who's flirting with the bass player—seem to want to be up in their rooms listening to the wind and rain when there's the distraction of company.

One by one, Pia lights the new candles. Her mother had made her attend mass as a child and the lighting of the wicks reminds her of those years of supplication, the smell of incense, the ease of ritual. Her mouth on the toes of the statue of the saviour, that gentle kiss.

And then she remembers the dog from the village by the sea—brown, a terrier of sorts, with perky ears. The dog was starving—her teats hanging sacs; fur patchy with mange. Pia fed her a scrap of meat in the yard—dry and tough from a stew her mother had made. The next day the dog was in the yard again and Pia fed her some greasy sausage stolen from the fridge, the dog licking Pia's fingers. On another occasion the dog leaned in and nuzzled Pia's cheek.

The terrier came to the yard four or five times that month—always tentative and warily watching the house. After the fifth or sixth visit Pia started to think of possible names for her, imagined holding her and brushing out her matted fur with a hairbrush—imagined her mother finally letting her have a dog.

One morning Pia and her mother left home to accompany Pia's father on a business trip. He had a series of meetings in a nearby city and Pia's mother wanted out of the village, even if it meant taking Pia with her. The gate closed behind them with a clang. They came home a week later. It was night and the sea was shushing quietly and the stars were out and a pickaxe of moon, and down below on the passeig people sat out on the patios. Tinny music came from a radio near a neighbour's open window. Pia's father was using his lighter to help his family see the way up the path. He kept burning his thumb and Pia remembers how her mother, who might normally have laughed at that, did not. When they got close to the door of the house, there was a stench. Raw, thick, spoiled. Pia's mother covered her face and went inside and Pia's father—with only the flame from his lighter—searched the yard between the gate and the door for what might be causing the smell, not noticing Pia was following him. He flicked the lighter again. Next to the pole for the laundry line was the dog's carcass, already picked apart by buzzards.

WHEN PIA WAS VERY YOUNG, her parents constantly debated about whether Pia and her mother should leave the village by the sea and return home, or wait until Pia's father's business arrangements were sorted out. After the house was looted, Pia's father paid privately for security. There was always a man—six over the years—in their yard or wandering into the kitchen to ask for a cup of coffee, a gun tucked into his belt. Sometimes it was a young cabo. There had been one in his twenties . . . Pia can still picture him wiping flakes of cocoa pastry and bits of sugar off the front of his shirt and looking at her sheepishly.

Pia was six when the kitchen help was let go and her mother taught her how to bake, and how to cook simple foods: rustic stews and grilled vegetables, spicy paellas made with local prawns. Some days Pia was allowed to go to the market or to the docks to buy fish, always with the cabo trailing behind her. Most days she was told to invent her own games, to entertain herself. This is just how it was—Pia never spoke about her loneliness to anyone, not even to her abuela, who, years later, would put her finger under her granddaughter's chin and ask, 'What's going on in that head of yours?' How to describe it? The village by the sea existed in a world where people were stunned by what they'd seen, where what you cooked with, how many prawns you could afford, said everything about your resources and your power.

And so Pia grew up to become someone who moved quietly, who studied other people's introspection; whose gaze followed theirs as she listened to what they said and

what they omitted. The men and women from her childhood in the village by the sea hadn't joked about anything.
They'd watched their own wrist bones becoming more
prominent daily; their hands shook when they waited at the
storehouse for rations, or when they were forced into begging. *This storm,* Pia thinks, as the wind buffets the hotel
walls, *is nothing.* Here we are in our stone building, here is
the food and the wine, here is the builder conferring with
the night clerk and wiping his hands on a white towel, and
here is the barman wagging an empty bottle of wine in the
air and asking the wedding party with a laugh, 'Come on
now, who's going to pay for this?' Here we are in our warm
clothes with no one coming to rape or kill us.

Pia stands up. She thinks about taking the nub of bread
and slip of Camembert back into the kitchen but instead she
gets up off the floor, says good night to everyone and walks
upstairs past the wallpaper with its rich striping, the globe
lamps with their dim amber light, the mirror on the landing.
One of the books she'd taken from the widow's library, one
of the books from her close-your-eyes-and-point game, was
a slim blue volume with no title on its spine and typewrit-
ten, not printed, pages. It began with a statement: *The water
is a mirror.* This was followed by:

> *The mirror is a semblance of self, a way of knowing.*
> *Mirrors are only preoccupied with their inhabitants*
>   *when they're awake.*
> *(This applies to both the mirrors and the inhabitants.)*

The world is a mirror. It will not remember us after we
pass through it.

Pia glances into the mirror on the landing as she passes and sees, through her exhaustion and the hum of the wine, a veiled face looking back at her. She opens her eyes wider, focusing. But it's just her own face—short dark hair, dark eyes: a woman close to the age her mother was when she was murdered, the resemblance startling.

A man sitting at a restaurant table once, in Pia's childhood village, had tired eyes like this, two half-moons of purple ink below them. Her mother had reached out and touched this man's hand, even though in those days she knew better than to reach out to anyone. '¿Triste?' Pia had asked, when they'd walked a distance away. Her mother bent down to her. 'Sí,' she said, 'sad.' And then she cupped Pia's cheek in her palm and asked, '¿Te gusta él? You like him?' And Pia squinted because she did like his face, his eyes as blue as the swimming pool she'd once seen in her mother's magazine. And her mother had looked back down the passeig to where the man was sitting and said, 'So don't forget him. This is all you can do.'

1 stand outside my room and peer down the hall toward the stairwell. The cabo, Alejandro, is nowhere to be seen, though he's rapped on my door hourly, calling out '¿Señor?' and waiting until I answer. When I neither see him nor hear him moving around on the ground floor I walk down the hall and knock lightly on Suzanne and Bernard's door. The hotel's hallway, with its blue paint and brass sconces, is a relic of the establishment's better days—those years before the civil war when the rooms were stocked with decent towels and bars of soap, and breakfast arrived under a polished silver cloche.

Suzanne answers the door in the brown dress she was wearing yesterday. For months she's alternated between this dress, and a pair of slacks and light sweater. She glances down the hall, then ushers me in. She's been staying in the same room as Bernard since he became ill in Marseilles, making sure he's resting properly and taking the sulphapyridine she sourced through an acquaintance in Narbonne. Bernard is lying in bed with a blanket tucked around him, a gleam of sweat on his forehead. He's only thirty-four, roughly the same age as Suzanne, but he's been steadily losing weight and his gauntness and jaundiced complexion make him appear a decade older. Beside him is the empty plate upon which the woman from the kitchen sent up bread and oil. It's after ten a.m. now, maybe closer to eleven. I'm losing track of time.

'I brought my bread,' I say, holding out the plate, 'if anyone wants it.'

Suzanne laughs. 'No croissants? God, but I wake up and go to bed picturing Madame Clément's patisserie window.'

'How is he?' I ask, nodding toward Bernard. Then I see that Bernard is awake and watching me and that I'm doing what most people do—what everyone did to my brother— enquiring about the ill or the infirm as if they aren't capable of answering for themselves.

'The same,' she says. 'I'm worried about his fever.'

'What did you bring us, professor?' Bernard's voice is thin and reedy.

I turn the plate of crusty bread in his direction.

'Ah, divine.' He frees an arm from under the blanket, picks the bread off the plate and then sets it back down. 'Are there no more of the olives you brought yesterday?'

Suzanne glares at me; my excursion angered her. I shake my head no. 'Did I tell you there was an art gallery too, in the square?'

'And to think you came back.' Bernard laughs.

'I'm not the one known to disappear,' I say—a reference to our years in Saint-Germain-des-Prés when Bernard was famous for his unexpected departures: a group of us would head out to an exhibit, or to a friend's house for dinner, only to discover we'd lost Bernard at some juncture in our travels. His decamping became so frequent we assumed he had a secret lover and was slipping away to be with him. Once, though, retracing my steps to where I'd last seen him, I found Bernard standing underneath the façade of a church, craning his neck to study the gargoyles studded over its fascia. His paintings, at that time, were dark—like a world painted at dusk or covered in ash. This image of him standing there in the last traces of the day's light was like that—his head angled back, the gargoyles pawing the air above him. 'Bernard!' I called, and he turned and raised a hand, and came toward me. Years later I thought I could see some semblance of those gargoyles in his street scenes—the wide eyes of the pedestrians; the boy with the wooden tureen, begging.

———

In my youth I devoted long stretches of time to social studies. For one enquiry I drew a number of maps of our family's country house. The house was not a grand one, but it came with property as my grandfather and his father before him owned and managed the wood lots that provided timber for the nearby villages. The house had a dozen rooms on the two main floors, as well as a subterranean kitchen and a small attic that sat behind a triangular gable and round window at the front. The main floor was comprised of communal spaces: an entry hall, a sitting room, a dining room, my father's study and library—which sometimes doubled as my laboratory—and a loggia that looked out over a tidy garden. The upper floors contained five bedrooms and a lavatory. My parents' bedroom was at the far end of the hall beside the nanny's room, my room was across from my parents', and Meira's room—the former nursery to which I'd once been confined—was across from Nanny Bette's. Our younger brother, Martin, was down the hall past the stairwell in a room hung with heavy green curtains capable of replicating the starkest hours of night in the middle of even the brightest summer day. Because Martin was ill throughout his childhood, he rarely caused the sort of trouble Meira and I did. I think if he'd been well he might not have been so docile, might have had Meira's temper, but instead he lay in a distant orbit on the outskirts of my family's day-to-day life. I'm ashamed to say it, but he was loved less than Meira and I were, as if my parents were too afraid to become attached to him. He died at seven, and even though we all wept, there was, for me, a sense that my parents' strategy had been correct and that we did not diminish as a family because of Martin's death, but turned toward each other with a renewed sense of commitment.

When I had drawn the maps of the house, Martin was still with us. As part of my experiment I measured the distance between the upstairs habitations and the various domains on the ground floor: the study my father spent his evenings in, the blue sitting room where my mother wrote letters and visited with guests, the cubby near the bay window where I was allowed to set up that day's selection of books . . . My map and measurements yielded a thesis which I wrote out in careful ink and tried to prove mathematically: the notion that affiliation is borne by proximity, and that proximity is requisite for love.

I sit at the foot of the bed and rest my hand on Bernard's leg. I think about what it would be like to have a younger brother at this advanced age and imagine I might feel toward him something close to what I feel for Bernard. In Paris, Bernard was often remote and I sometimes found him intolerably selfish, but when we met again at Gaston's flat just before my internment our commonalities outweighed our differences. For reasons I have yet to fully fathom, it was Bernard, out of all our circle of friends, who did the most to try to secure my release from the camp in Nevers: gathering affidavits to give to the commission charged with reviewing the cases of foreign nationals, securing the support of six prominent academics who would not have recognized the poorly dressed artist knocking at their door and who would not have opened it save for his insistence. In the camp des travailleurs volontaires, we were allowed to send only two letters a week and allowed to keep no more than twenty francs. That was sixteen letters over two months. Were it not for Bernard's visits and his work on my behalf, I might still be there on my bed of straw. I think now of the work a letter took, writing in those crowded rooms, or in the courtyard under the bowl of bad weather. How to ask for favours? How to make a case for myself and my work? This has always been an issue with me. It takes five hundred words, a thousand words to say, *Would you please help?* yet I didn't have to ask Bernard at all.

After my release from the camp, I returned to the library and my research, though with more uncertainty than ever before. Again it was Bernard who kept coming to my flat and saying we must leave Paris. Meira was already in America, sending letters I did not receive and calling around to friends who had telephones to ask them to deliver me messages. Always, the message was *Go*. I knew in late May it was time, and not because Gaston told us that Auteuil and Passy were already abandoned—the sixteenth arrondissement's consulates and embassies, the manors, dark at all hours . . . even the birdcage in the window of one stately house with its grilled door gaping open—but rather because of the archivist at the Bibliothèque Nationale. Strange that I should forget his name when I can conjure his face so readily: his bulbous nose and squint eyes, the dark threads of hair across the top of his head thin and distinct, like the lines on an empty sheet of music. Michel! That's it! It was Michel who told me, without words, to leave. He had been at his desk less and less often, and when I last saw him, after waiting impatiently for some manuscript or book I had requested days before, he was scuttling about with a large and unwieldy stack of papers. Libraries are places of precision; this stack and the ones that followed signalled that he had been tasked with moving the library's most important documents to safety. I went home that afternoon, taking a long and circuitous route through the city, past two small parks and the Jardin du Luxembourg, which stretched off over my right shoulder like paradise. I walked through my local market, waved at the butcher, stood for a moment at the busy corner outside my patisserie and then went in, as was customary on my return home, to buy one perfect cake orange. Nina, always at work on the weekday, placed it in a small box with as much care as she might a great cake that would serve ten. 'À demain,' she said, as if this would happen again and again. That night I began to sort through my papers.

'Dreaming again?' Bernard teases.

I relax my mouth, can feel my face set in the pensive expression he'd been studying. 'Do you think you'll be all right when Suzanne and I go to the station?' I ask.

'I'll be fine.' As if to prove his point, he pushes himself up so that he's sitting with his back against the wooden headboard. He struggles more than he'd like, but his smile, at the end of the effort, is still boyishly victorious.

I look at Suzanne, who's standing just inside the open balcony inspecting the cuffs of her dress. She has lines on her forehead and around her mouth that I don't remember from the few times we'd met in Paris.

'We won't be long,' she says to Bernard. 'It's better if you stay behind, anyway—if we all go they can put us on a train back to France with no questions asked. If you stay and they decide to deport us, at least that buys us time to come back here and gather our things . . .' She trails off, glancing around the room as if she's forgotten where she set a pair of gloves or a favourite scarf.

'How do I look?' she eventually asks, holding her arms out from her sides. Her hair is damp from washing it, and falls softly over her shoulders and catches the light; the spots where she's scrubbed her cuffs are still wet and I peer more closely to see if they look clean. We have hours before the appointment—hours in which Alejandro, like the cog in a clock, will regularly pester us to affirm our presence—but already we're preparing. Suzanne steps fully into the room. Outside, above the balcony, the gulls squawk and swoop down toward the promenade, arguing over some scrap of food.

While we wait for our appointment Suzanne is given permission to make a few calls from the hotel lobby, albeit at a significant cost. Twenty minutes later she is back in the room, her face serious. What Porras told us seems to be true—they're sending anyone with a visa from Marseilles back, though one of Suzanne's contacts has heard that the border is temporarily closed to everyone. 'As of yesterday,' she tells us, pulling the writing-table chair out into the middle of the room and taking a seat.

Bernard rubs his eyes and surveys the side table where his pills are. 'I could use a cigarette.'

'You only have six left,' Suzanne says. 'Wait until you're better.'

'So do we bribe someone?' Bernard asks.

Suzanne gets up, walks over to her purse, lights one of her own cigarettes and passes it to Bernard. After a minute she says, 'It could be fine. Maybe Marco will be there, maybe they'll honour the transit visas already issued, regard-less of where they're from. Or maybe this is just a ploy to refuse people with legitimate papers. Make it someone else's problem.' She uses the word 'legitimate' even though one of my papers—a residency card—and one of Bernard's are forged. The American Foreign Service had also issued me a new passport in Marseilles. It was legitimate but identified me as Austrian—which we'd say was a clerical mistake if anything came of it. I didn't want to test this, though; it wouldn't take much to discover that I was, in fact, German.

Suzanne smooths her skirt and studies the calluses on her palms. 'What do we think would sway Porras?'

Bernard pushes himself farther up against the headboard of his bed. 'He won't give us anything. He's a fascist.'

'Can we leave now without our papers?' Suzanne looks from Bernard to me.

'Back over the mountain?' I ask.

Suzanne shrugs.

'Not possible,' I say. Even if the guard would take a bribe—and I suspect he won't—neither Bernard nor I would make it over the col in our current state. Even Suzanne is flagging; she's had little to eat over the past two days: a wedge of bread, some chicken soup, a half-dozen olives. And if we did manage to cross back into France we would almost surely be detained. Any stop in France—at the stations, outside the embassies, or sometimes even on the streets—means showing identity papers, which for us means showing up empty-handed and hoping that the man or woman looking at us is ignorant, or tired, or willing to help people they shouldn't be assisting.

Suzanne, too, eventually dismisses the idea of a bribe or escape. Bernard is too weak and the Spanish are unpredictable. She says that she thinks she can make a case for us. She says, wearily, that if we were on any sort of extradition list we'd be locked up already, or dead, and not out on our balconies with a pock-faced twenty-year-old guarding the lobby door. I'm less convinced. I've felt a gutting certainty since yesterday that we'll be sent back across the border. If we say we can afford the train, we'll be escorted to the station and handed over to a guard who will accompany us to Cerbère, where he'll hand us over to a French guard with limited ability to help. If we say we can't afford the train, they'll walk us back up the mountain and stop at the ridge near the border stone that identifies a donkey who brays in one language from a donkey who brays in another. They'll leave us in a set of pastures so remote they might shoot us in the back for the sport of it, or to save them the trouble of wondering if we'll turn around after an hour's walk and try to cross the border again.

'Professor?' Bernard asks. 'What are you thinking?'

I reach out and tap his knee. For a moment, I can almost imagine telling him that I'm thinking I need a jug in order to kill myself, that the thought of prison, or of covering long distances again under my own volition places me beyond despair. Instead I look over my spectacles into his eyes and say, 'Gargoyles.'

I HAPPEN UPON ALEJANDRO at the base of the stairs. I gather from his heavy-lidded eyes that he's been napping on the overstuffed sofa, and only sprung up when he heard me coming down.

'I'm looking for a jug,' I say. 'For water.'

Alejandro surveys the hotel lobby as if it's slowly coming into focus: the sofa, end tables, threadbare cabriole chairs, the potted palms flanking the sideboard with its delicate lace runner, the marble reception desk.

I gesture toward the archway that leads to the kitchen and walk in that direction. Alejandro falls into step behind me and then stops abruptly as if it's occurred to him that this might be a ruse—Suzanne and Bernard sneaking out behind me, perhaps. He glances over his shoulder at the empty room, then strides up to the swinging door to the kitchen, calls out '¿Hola?' and pushes the door open.

Inside the kitchen, the radio is on, trumpets and trombones cheerfully sounding over wind instruments and a drum. This is music of the people—music I find too homey in dangerous times. The smell of boiled potato and herbs permeates the room even though there's no pot on the stove. I'm suddenly famished.

Alejandro calls again and the widow—the old proprietress who reluctantly gave us rooms two days ago and who argued with Alejandro when he escorted us back from the station yesterday—appears through a second doorway at the far end of the room. Her grey hair is twisted into a coil, her expression well rehearsed in its neutrality. She wipes her hands on her apron and waits for Alejandro to speak.

'Un favor,' Alejandro says, gesturing in my direction even as he's watching the lobby from the doorway.

I ask for une cruche, explaining that there's no jug in my room and I need to wash. The proprietress narrows her eyes as if she suspects that the room had been equipped with a jug when I arrived.

'¡Rapidament!' Alejandro claps.

The proprietress glares at him with the full force of her disdain. These may be dangerous times but that doesn't mean she'll allow herself to be clapped at by a twenty-year-old who grew up in the next village over.

In what appears to be a purposefully slow process, the

proprietress gathers a wooden footstool and then climbs up on it in order to inspect a series of cupboards that run along the wall over the counter. Some contain stacked glasses, some teacups. One cupboard is filled with single-stem flower vases, another with dessert glasses for ice cream sundaes. When all of those cupboards have been checked, the proprietress drags the footstool over to a tall cabinet. The top two shelves hold an array of dishes that seem not to be in use. A blue ceramic jug is lifted out from behind a stack of plates. Alejandro takes the jug from the proprietress and peers inside it. Satisfied that nothing untoward is being passed between us, he hands it to me. There's a large chip along the vessel's rim and another at the base of the scroll handle where the potter had shaped a little flourish. The jug is the colour of the sea at night—the same dark blue of the poet's coat in one of Bernard's best portraits.

'¿Bé?' Alejandro asks.

For a second, this jug and his 'okay?' feel like a kind of permission, two small marks of progress that will eventually add up to the fact of my no longer existing. I take the jug and turn toward the sitting room thinking about the poet's coat, and of another poet who wrote, in the last year of his life, about ancient feasts and finding his appetite again just as he was dying. I am inhaling boiled potato and herbs and remembering the taste of butter and gravy, and feeling ashamed that in the past few months I've dreamt about food more often than I've dreamt about my family or the people I love. And suddenly my heartbeat is welling in my ears, and the floor slips out from under me. I reach out but there's nothing to grab, only Alejandro whose arm flies out to catch me. The jug slipping out of my hand and smashing at my feet—though the noise of this comes from far off, like a calamity in a distant room.

'Monsieur?'

I open my eyes to the lobby's plaster ceiling. Alejandro is seated beside me on the sofa with his hands on my shoulders. I realize he's been shaking me and that this shaking is what's woken me. He's taken off his cap and his black curls are flattened where the band has exerted the most pressure. I clear my throat, try to sit up properly. 'Pardon,' I say, thinking only of my room, of rest, sleep. But then I remember the jug breaking into pieces on the tile floor.

Alejandro turns to the table beside the sofa and picks up a white bowl. In it is a modest ladling of the broth I smelled in the kitchen—potato and steaming meat and a piquant of pepper, a trace of sage or thyme. It smells like childhood, like the closeness inside my brother's room where he was often fed meals to save him from the exertion of coming down to the dining room, and where twice a week I went in after dinner to read to him.

'Eat,' Alejandro says. This close, there are flecks of gold in his brown eyes, and his nostrils flare elegantly, reminding me of Salomé's Arabian horses. He lifts the spoon to my mouth, his hand trembling.

———

When I wake up later in the grey light of my room, Suzanne is standing at the foot of my bed. Behind her the sky is a late-afternoon blue, accented by a few lazy clouds moving across the bay.

'Well, it seems you're no good, either,' she says. 'It's a miracle the two of you made it over the col.'

There's tension in her voice under the veil of amiability, reminding me of how Salomé spoke to me at the end of our affair.

'So,' Suzanne continues, 'the guard—'

'—Alejandro,' I say.

'Yes, well, the new plan is this: *Alejandro* will stay here to make sure you and Bernard don't try to crawl your way to Portugal, and I'm being escorted to meet the station supervisor on our mutual behalf.' She reaches down and squeezes my foot where my toes have made a tent under the thin white blanket. 'I'll do my best not to abandon you.'

'And if it doesn't work out?' I ask.

'We'll take the train back to France, try to get through the first inspection with our papers, wait a few days at Leon's, make some phone calls, and try again.' She says this casually, as if we'd be let free upon arrival on the other side. 'We're not the only ones in this situation,' she adds. 'There will be others at the border, the station will be busy.' Again, a near-smile; I know this is the most she can muster. I try to smile back, though this idea that there is safety in numbers is a lie, which is beneath her.

Suzanne smooths her hair over her shoulder, as if she's setting out for an evening with friends. 'Get some rest.' She squeezes my foot again and walks around to the side of the bed, kisses me on my forehead. On her way to the door she sees my notebook open on the side table.

'Are you working?' she asks lightly.

I push myself up into a sitting position so I have a better view of the sea. 'Daydreams,' I say, and lightly wave my hand in the air.

AFTER I'VE RESTED, I GO TO SIT with Bernard in his room. He's standing by the balcony when I enter, looking toward the sea, just as I have been doing most of the day. Again I note how much weight he's lost: his trousers baggy, belt cinched tightly, brown sweater hanging like a sack. When he turns to me I see that he's smoking and this makes me happy for him—that he can choose certain activities for himself.

'I've been thinking about Salomé,' I say.

'The red mare?' Bernard laughs and eases himself into a chair by the balcony railing. He'd come up with this endearment after he'd started painting her in Paris, well before the war. The painting was a commission from her father, which was Salomé's way of giving Bernard money without it appearing to be a handout. I saw the painting once in its early stages: Salomé in a black and cream kimono draping ever so slightly off her shoulder; an oriental vase filled with poppies on the table beside her. He burned the painting later, as I recall, believing it to be derivative.

Bernard takes a drag from his cigarette and blows the smoke toward the open sky. 'Last I heard she was with that Russian she'd taken up with in Trieste.'

I lean on the railing and look toward the mountain, a darkening outline against a dusky sky. Below us, grape pickers coming off the hillside terraces are making their way home.

'Do you remember her friend?' Bernard asks. 'The painter who was working on bowls of fruit. *Only* bowls of fruit?' Bernard peers gently into my face, brows furrowed, his eyes lively. '"Not even a bottle of claret?" I asked him, "no draping cloth, no vase? What of the onion? The dead-eyed fish?"' Bernard laughs. '"Where's your rooster?" I asked.' Bernard brings his cigarette to his lips, inhales, inspects the cinders before exhaling. 'He was right of course, which we all knew. The wood bowl, the wood table, three or four oranges, their dimpled skin . . . and Giorgio—that was his name, wasn't it?—too arrogant to even paint us a window.' Bernard laughs and tries to mask a cough.

'What would you paint here?' I ask, gesturing to the cove of Portbou, the sea tapping the shore, the headlands heavy as bookends.

'That's like me asking you what you'd write.' He stubs out his cigarette on the wrought-iron railing and flicks the butt toward the sea, shrugging deeper into his sweater. 'There are days I think I'll never have the courage to look at the world through a painter's eyes again.'

We don't talk of what's to come. We speak only about the past, but not idealistically. This is Bernard's refusal. Even in better days he was like this: he would add the hanging thread on the shawl of the woman he was painting, or show his model's exhaustion when she'd been sitting on a chair in a cold studio playing Ophelia for eight hours, because to ignore that exhaustion would be a lie. This cost him exhibitions I think, patrons who didn't want to be presented with scuffs on shoes, flowers dead in buttonholes.

It was Bernard who'd introduced me to Salomé. First in Paris on the street outside the Mogador—a meeting she could never remember—and then, again, a few months later at her family home in Vienna. By then Bernard had become one of her protégés—the invitation to Vienna, complete with rail tickets, was typical of Salomé's favours: invitations, a series of well-placed introductions, a few small commissions. The guests in Vienna were people she knew well: writers, artists, philosophers, members of what would soon become the Vienna Circle, former lovers and current lovers. The house was absurdly opulent. There were dancers with flaming batons on the lawn when we arrived and a doorman dressed as a harlequin. I could see Salomé enjoyed this show. At the start of dinner she rang her spoon against her glass, made a charming speech. When the wine ran low she sent a sculptor who didn't have two pfennigs to rub together down to the wine cellar with the key. 'Choose anything,' she said.

Everyone vied for her attention that evening. Here and there throughout the meal, pockets of jocular laughter would bubble up as if to entice her to look over. I was seated so far down the table I couldn't hear a word of her circle's conversation, and was left instead to discuss railways with a man from Pest, a student who was plodding in his thought. I remember the candles—how excessive they were, arranged all the way down the table, how they swayed when I stood up after too much wine. Salomé's father was a Russian manufacturer who had a taste for French tapestries and Chinese vases and hunting, and her mother was a renowned actress from Prague. There was a blurry photograph of the mother, posing as Scheherazade, on the mantel in the sitting room. She had the same snake of thick auburn hair as Salomé, the same deep-set eyes rimmed in kohl. But where Salomé had a petulant upturned nose, her mother had a long, delicate nose that flared at the tip, giving her the bearing of an aristocrat.

Toward the end of the night, the conversations in the stuffy drawing room became repetitive: Lenin, the Greek Republic, the fascists, the role of the arts in perilous times. It seemed as though every philosophy student in the room had taken up a position next to Salomé for a time, then returned to other conversations earnestly repeating what she'd said. And so, bored and light-headed, I slipped out of the house to walk the grounds. The mist was heavy and the world felt to me in that hour like something behind a curtain: plane after plane of the lawn, the statues appearing in relief. Across a gravel walkway I came upon a row of evergreen trees pruned into absurd shapes, and then a fountain circled by cherubs, water burbling through the winged figures' mouths. When I turned back at the stables, Salomé was standing there, no fur, no cover, her bare shoulders damp, her bony clavicles ghostly in the night.

'I always say,' she began, 'that it's the interesting ones who leave.' She walked toward me then and when we were close she kissed me on one cheek and then the other. She smelled like the essence my father sometimes brought back for my mother in a glass vial from the Middle East: wood, smoke, spice. 'Salomé,' she said as she took my arm, as if I didn't already know how her mouth tweaked when she was bored or her eyebrows shot up in delight. 'Now tell me everything you know about categorical imperatives. Bernard says you're brilliant and I can't get a straight answer out of anyone.'

We were lovers for a month after we returned to Paris. I stopped reading, stopped writing. Instead I paced: I waited for her to send a message to my dingy flat on Rue Dombasle or waited outside her studio like a beggar. Everyone warned me off her. 'She has a dozen lovers; she can be cruel.' But in those hours when she had only one, and it was me, we laughed as much as I'd ever laughed with anyone. She taught me tenderness. In a number of ways she made me: teased me out of myself, shaped me—though I understand now that she knew she was doing it, doing it for me, and to me, as she'd done for others. That was part of her allure—that always self-satisfied giving of the teacher: an exercise of power under the veneer of equality. In some ways I think I sensed this: how she always told me when to arrive, when to go. And that was how I knew, walking Rue Marmontel at four a.m.—dispatched back to my flat—that she had me. So I proposed to her the next evening in her studio, sloppily drunk and stupidly inarticulate. Caught up in the moment, I promised a ring I knew I couldn't afford. I muttered something about my father's estate—a bribe that sounded hollow and unappealing even to my ears. It would have been better if she'd laughed or taken pity on me there and then, but she didn't. Instead, she stood coolly, her skin lit blue in the light, likely ranking my proposal against innumerable overtures presented in that very room, in similar circumstances. I remember how I looked for something solid to hold on to, my eyes landing on the bed, the adjacent dressers and mirror; how the hound was so bored by the whole production, she was licking herself noisily in the corner of the room. I knew Salomé wouldn't say yes. And I knew, in some primal part of my brain, that in the very act of proposing I was willing her to end it because it had become too much for me. And so, she did. Slipped her red tunic over her head and, arms still raised as the silk fell around her shoulders, announced that she was going to Berlin with Lebedev, her favourite suitor. She would be gone at least a month. She called the dog, using some Russian pet name, and the grey beast sprang up and went to stand beside her, and the two of them left the room.

I have a scar on my forearm: a thin line of white skin, arcing like the tail of a comet. It's from that time after Salomé, a time that is almost inexplicable to me from the vantage point of these years, this hotel room. When I look back on the man I was then—twenty-eight years old and toying the tip of a knife against my skin—I don't recognize him, but for the urge to erase, to get away from a feeling I'm now mature enough to call futility.

After a period of silence Bernard walks over to the basin on the sideboard and splashes his face with water. His small pack, near empty save for a second set of clothes, sits on the chaise by the far wall of the room while Suzanne's even smaller bag is clasped in the dark mouth of the closet.

'Well,' Bernard says, drying his face, 'do we dare wonder what's taking Suzanne so long?'

On the passeig below us, the sound of a girl's laughter lilts skyward, its levity a shock. How long has it been since I've heard someone laugh so unabashedly?

I turn to Bernard. I raise my shoulders, fan out my hands. *I have nothing, I know as little about what Suzanne is facing as you do.* I desperately want to go out onto the street, want to see the girl who is laughing. In my heart that girl is you, Pia—but I'm stuck where I'm standing. I sense, then, that I ought to go back to my own room; that Bernard would prefer to be alone. As would I.

Back in my room I roll up my shirtsleeves and pick up a pen. It occurs to me that the reason I made that long arc with a knife up my forearm all those years ago was to prove something to myself: that the most impressionable things, the truest things, occur in solitude.

You will not need anyone, Pia. You will not stand by a stuttering fountain waiting for someone to drift in through the mist. You will be that rare and beautiful thing: someone who can give love without being constrained by the need to receive it.

I WENT TO YOUR ISLAND ONCE, Pia—this was a few months after I submitted my dissertation. What had started out as an analysis of German Idealism held up against Plato's world of forms had transformed itself into a relatively slim volume on bridges: what it means to span, to give shape to space, to transport. My favourite chapter—if one is allowed such a thing in one's own work—was on the Petit Pont in Paris. The most humble of the Seine's bridges, the Petit Pont connects the Île de la Cité to the Left Bank via a single stone archway. I had meant to use this bridge as an example of the problem of universals—the current Petit Pont is but the most recent of many prior Petit Ponts to span that part of the Seine since antiquity—but rather than investigating the obdurate properties of the bridge itself I became obsessed by its history, by the dozens of wood or stone Petit Ponts that were swept away by floods, broken up in storms, or destroyed by fire. I became obsessed, I suppose, by hauntings—the echo of time in our thinking. My dissertation was a failure, of course—I was summoned to the office of a senior professor, who waved me toward a wingback chair. He lit a pipe and turned to a window that overlooked the botanical gardens. His plump cheeks flexed in silence for ten minutes. Finally he cleared his throat and said, 'Add something. If you want to bring us the unexpected, this—' and here he turned and gestured to the typed pages on his desk, 'this *cogitation* . . . add the thing even you wouldn't expect to find to your deliberation. As yet there's no tension in it, nothing gets worked out.' He sat in his chair and looked at me thought-fully before taking off his glasses to wipe away some distor-tion on the lens. I felt as if everything was moving in slow motion. His glasses clear, the professor picked up a pen and began scratching out some notes. I intuited this had nothing to do with me. Eventually I stood to go, and at the creak of my chair he glanced up as if he'd forgotten I was there. 'Your handling of Fichte is also inadequate.' He nodded toward the door, his dissatisfaction no longer hidden, and went back to his work. I walked past his secretary without meeting her gaze and staggered toward my tenement in Sprengelkiez feeling like I'd been physically struck. I wanted to scream, but nothing, not even a whimper, came out. As soon as I was inside the door of my flat I kicked over a chair and swept three shelves of books to the floor.

After that I borrowed money from my father and went travelling to find the thing I hadn't thought about. I went far west, to the point where there were no more bridges, only boats, and then I travelled west again until I reached another coast and a series of sea-bedded islands. I paid for passage on a small mail steamer and sat through a rough journey in the clerk's cabin with five other passengers who took turns being sick in a wooden bucket one of the crew had left for us. I had three empty notebooks in my bag and clothes that were unsuited for the continual dampness of the weather. We docked at dawn on the south end of a hare-shaped island and made our way shakily up the pier toward a cluster of horse carts stationed at the top of the slipway. Behind the horse carts there were two cars. One of the drivers was willing to transport me and another passenger for a small fee, to which we both readily agreed. The road out of town was in poor condition, but the landscape was astounding: the rust reds and bog orange of a fertile earth, a world that seemed to be turning itself over; the ground thick-coated like some sort of pelt. I think I could have cried—from the relief of the island's remoteness—were I not riding with a man who kept trying to speak to me about pharmaceuticals. 'Good health,' he announced, 'depends on a number of factors. Exercise,' he said, raising a thin finger, 'ample nutrients'—another finger shot up—'and tonics to cleanse.' His case of wares bumped up and down on the seat beside him, its little vials tinkling. He left us at the largest town in the middle of the island and at last I was alone in the back of the car, listening as the driver, a local entrepreneur who offered his automotive services for the return journey, pointed out the loch, and an old parish church, and a rugged field where a circle of stones once stood. I was dropped off at the edge of the village not far from the hotel just as the sun nudged up above the fields. The gentleman's car reversed noisily in a wide section of track. Up ahead, whitewashed cottages lined both sides of the road, but where I stood there was nothing but field, bracken and bog on one side, and a grassy ledge that dropped toward the sea on the other.

Here in Portbou, the church bells ring. I'm sitting at the foot of my bed when they chime five o'clock. Outside, the sky is turning dusky, but not like it would on your island, Pia—this Mediterranean dusk tends toward a saxe blue, as if a sloppy painter has washed the sea up into the horizon. Suzanne has been gone well over an hour, so I walk back to Bernard's room and together we imagine the possibilities. I tell him that I think one or both of our names has appeared on an extradition list and that Suzanne has been detained, but Bernard will not hear of it.

'They'd have come for us already.' His tone is dismissive, but I can tell he's anxious. 'It could be my identity paper from Paris,' he says. 'It hasn't been renewed, but Suzanne can explain that. Everything else is in order.'

I smile. Nothing is in order. Nothing has been in order since we left Paris and joined the march south. No matter where we stand, the ground shifts beneath us. At least my transit visas are in my name, but even though the stamps on them are real, they're only valid for three more days.

Bernard moves toward the little desk opposite the bed and sits sideways on the simple chair in front of it. If he weren't so gaunt he would look silly, like a man at a child's desk.

'We should have gone farther inland,' I say, 'kept walking.'

Bernard shakes his head—the question of when to present

ourselves is a debate we'd had days earlier. 'No,' he says, 'it was better to arrive with the others.' He looks up at the ceiling light, the dead flies lining the bottom of its glass globe. 'If only our contact—if only this "Marco" had been at the station.'

We have resolved to go downstairs and make enquiries with Alejandro when we hear the muffled sound of a knock on a door down the hall. Bernard runs his hands over his head—a habit from before the war when he had soft brown curls. I can feel my body's heaviness, its lethargy—so unlike those months in Paris and Marseilles when even the squeak of a floorboard started my pulse racing.

'¿Señor?' Alejandro calls, rapping on the door to my empty room.

Bernard sticks his head out into the hall. 'Ici,' he says, and gestures toward his room. A second later Alejandro is in front of us, his eyes narrowed in reprimand.

'Entrez,' Bernard says and Alejandro steps into the room with a level of formality that, under different circumstances, would be amusing: the rigid posture, raised chin. He stands stiffly just inside the door, as if he's entered a private house with fine carpets and art instead of a room with threadbare blankets and dead moths along the floorboards.

'Your presence has been requested by the commissioner,' Alejandro says. He holds a small square of paper in his hand, and glances at it as if it's proof of this communiqué. 'If you would come with me.'

———

I expected, as we walked out the front door of the hotel, that we would be turning toward La Rambla de Catalunya—the route to the police station—but instead Alejandro indicates that we are to turn right onto the Passeig de la Sardana. The street is busier than it was during my outing yesterday. Gone is the mineral lilt of the sea I'd savoured as I'd walked along; now there is only the odd fug of cigarette smoke as men return home from their offices or sit on restaurant patios having a drink. It gives me some pleasure, as we walk, to look at the locals' faces. Every now and again we pass one or two people who seem almost content, who have somehow managed to come through the worst of the civil war intact. At one of the larger cafés, two young men in white shirts are smiling. Next to them, a father listens attentively to his young son. Normally, today would be a school day—though I'm unsure if the schools are running here again. And that thought, of education, of the tide of the world's knowledge still churning, strikes me as insane—like naming the parts of a house as it crumbles. How will that boy remember these years? What will his catalogue of images be? How do you teach from within the centre of what is barbaric?

The boy's father senses that he's being watched and glances up toward the street, but when he sees Bernard and me being escorted by a guard in uniform, he immediately busies himself with some object on the table in front of him. Shortly after this Alejandro picks up the pace and Bernard and I fall behind. Alejandro turns and glares at us. I imagine there's no honour in parading us through town and that he'd prefer to make quick work of it. I stop walking out of sheer obstinacy and Alejandro comes back to face me.

'Where are we going?' I ask.

Alejandro doesn't reply. He's staring over my shoulder at one of the café patios, his face anxious. I turn to the café to discern the cause of his unease but before I can track the subject of his attention—the trio of girls with black hair, the young man alone with a beer—Alejandro says 'We're almost there' and starts off again, though more slowly this time. When we reach La Dorada with its bougainvillea wreathing the archway and its yellow door, Alejandro turns in. Even before he opens the door, I see Suzanne through the window, sitting with four men at a round table in the centre of the room—her dress and hair elegant in the globed light, though I know there is a tear on her sleeve and that the stains along the cuff didn't wash out. As we enter, she tosses her head back in laughter.

'Commissioner,' Alejandro says, saluting a plump man in a navy business suit—plump as only a government official with connections to the black market can be.

The commissioner stands up and shakes Bernard's hand, then mine. 'My name is Camilo Estévez,' he says. 'Please sit.' He indicates two empty chairs at the table, opposite Suzanne. We take our seats and I look to Suzanne for a cue but her eyes tell us nothing. 'Of course you know Señor Porras, who met you yesterday at the station?' the commissioner continues.

Señor Porras nods.

'And this,' Commissioner Estévez extends his hand to the towheaded man beside Porras, 'is Herr Gabler, a guest in our country. And here, beside me, is my friend Señor Noguerra.' The commissioner places his hand on the shoulder of a middle-aged man in a grey suit. 'He's out of uniform just now, but I think you will forgive him.'

I look at Bernard. He is following the round of introductions but says nothing. Instead he lifts his linen napkin and places it across his lap.

'We were just being delighted by your friend here,' the commissioner says, taking his seat again before turning to address Señor Porras in Spanish.

'Of course,' Porras replies, making a little shooing gesture at Alejandro. Our guard excuses himself and takes up a stool at the marble-topped bar at the far end of the restaurant.

'What would you like?' the commissioner asks jovially. 'I'm sorry to hear you've both been unwell. The least we can do for guests in our country is feed them.' He hands Bernard and me menus and waves his fingers in the air for the waiter. There are three other occupied tables in the restaurant behind him: two sets of men drinking coffee, and a wealthy couple in their fifties. None of them raise their eyes toward us.

Suzanne has a glass of wine in front of her, and the men have coffees and some sort of dark brown liquor. The commissioner takes a drink of his, then drops his glass down with a thud. 'The merienda is very good here. For you, sir?' he asks me. 'Some cured meat perhaps? Bread? Cheese? The olives are wonderful as well, from the local groves.'

Herr Gabler laughs at this. I notice now that he's wearing a black uniform like those of the SS agents we saw south of Paris.

'Have you had the lamb, commissioner?' Porras asks, and then he leans toward Suzanne and whispers something in her ear. She smiles and laughs politely and lifts her glass, knocking her elbow lightly against the table edge. A splash of wine spills on the tablecloth, and when the men on either side of Suzanne lean in with napkins to blot the stain, she looks at Bernard and me with wide eyes as if to say she has no idea why we're here or what's transpiring.

Bernard clears his throat and juts out his chin. 'Is it possible to order a bottle?' he asks cheerfully, and for a second I see the old healthy Bernard holding court at the foot of a table of artists in a Paris restaurant. He surveys the menu. I see exactly what he's doing and act accordingly: I imagine I am back home at a dinner party, where I belong. This, I know, will have been Suzanne's ruse as well—to act as if we have no cause to be frightened.

An elderly waiter with tufty grey eyebrows leans over to serve our wine, shakily wiping the bottle's lip on a linen cloth between pours. He's undoubtedly a local—he has the same colouring as Señor Porras and Señor Noguerra, their eyes dark and quick, their accents similar. Porras, the architect of this meeting, leans toward Suzanne, making recommendations on the menu while conferring with the waiter: *Is it too early for food? Ah, but our guests are hungry now.* 'This,' he says to Suzanne, pointing to her menu, 'is—' and then he kisses his fingers with his lips.

Commissioner Estévez, the senior figure at the table, laughs, chiding Porras in Spanish, saying that it's too early for a full meal but surely the owner will accommodate his guests with some small plates. He switches to English, asks Suzanne 'What time do you have supper in France?'

'Whenever we want,' Suzanne replies, and the slightly flirtatious tone of her comment lights up the men's faces. We are suddenly neck-deep in the farce, in this amplified comedy. More wine is poured. I look again at the tables of locals sitting between us and the door: common people, working people drinking coffee, nibbling on sandwiches. People struggling to pretend we're not here, in the middle of the room, ordering extravagant food—as conspicuous as a circus act.

Bernard lets out a laugh, light and quick, at something Herr Gabler says in his rustic French, and I see Alejandro, over at the bar, dare a quick glance over his shoulder. Our eyes meet and I feel something in the exchange; some form of alliance.

'Now then—' Commissioner Estévez says, placing his arms and elbows on the table and leaning forward, 'no one has asked me what I'm the commissioner of.' He smiles first at Suzanne and then at me and Bernard. 'It's a simple question and we're all friends.' I note, in his smile, the health of his teeth, that his moustache is thick, well groomed, and as grey as the hair on his head. 'But first we should agree on a language, don't you think? Herr Gabler's

Spanish is not so good and his English is frightening. And my German is, well . . .' He waves his right hand in the air as if swatting at a fly.

'Sprechen Sie Deutsch?' Herr Gabler asks me.

'Je préfère parler en français,' I say, lifting my wine to my lips.

'Of course we speak some German,' Suzanne says in English. 'Most Austrians and educated French people do. We also speak some Hungarian.'

'So we will convene in Hungarian?' the commissioner asks, and he laughs. Señor Porras and Herr Gabler laugh with him, but less enthusiastically than before.

The waiter comes toward the table then with eight small plates on a wide silver tray. Behind him, the locals finally turn their heads our way. This is black market food: cured chorizo, cuts of beef, even the butter on the mound of steaming vegetables is rare these days. I recall how walking back to the hotel yesterday, I'd passed by a beggar who was clearly starving. How I gave her a few of my olives.

The beef is placed in front of Suzanne—four rare strips that she will find hard to digest after months on the barest of rations. The vegetables are arranged in the middle of the table with a silver serving spoon, the lamb and fish dishes between Herr Gabler and us. The chorizo is placed in front of Commissioner Estévez, who beckons the waiter closer with one finger to give further instructions. The waiter totters off, and the commissioner returns his attention to Bernard and me.

'Shall we pray first?' he asks jokingly. 'Who will lead us?'

Señor Noguerra and Señor Porras exchange glances. Both claim to be officers of the Guardia Civil but only Porras is in the grey-green uniform of the security forces, its silver monogram pinned to his collar. Still, the two men seem well acquainted with each other, and share the local accent, whereas Commissioner Estévez's Spanish and his bearing belong to someone who comes from a different part of the country—perhaps a large city, I think, judging by his impatience.

'You must be wondering about our host,' Porras says evenly, as if he too is suddenly tired of the charade. 'Commissioner Estévez is the Commissioner of Information. He's on a tour of the border areas.'

'Beautiful country—' the commissioner interjects, raising a pronged piece of meat to his mouth.

'He's responsible,' Porras continues, 'for international crimes and for identity documents.' Porras reaches into the pocket of his uniform and drops fourteen documents on the table between his knife and fork. Suzanne's light blue identity card from Paris is on top and the yellow folded bits of paper that are our Spanish transit visas are underneath. My passport, which gives me Austrian citizenship, is on the bottom.

We say nothing, and in that silence Porras pulls a cigarette from his silver case and a lighter. He flicks the lighter into flame. He could burn those papers now, and we three could stand up shouting, and no one would do a thing. The waiter returns with another bottle of wine. He shows the commissioner the label, then takes the capsule off with the blade of a knife. I watch the peel of metal fall to the table. Suzanne stares down at her untouched beef.

'Why is everyone suddenly so serious?' the commissioner asks. 'Eat! Eat!'

On my parents' property in the country there were a number of woodsheds out in the forest amongst the trees. My father, and his father before him, were responsible for them. When I was seven or eight I would sometimes visit one. It had a door, which was never locked, and a small window covered by a flap of burlap. Inside there was a pyramid of logs and some basic tools and woodcutting implements. And of course, years later, my cousin Leonie and I would be in there too, and my mother with her startled face, white as the moon above us. This was a place where I sometimes stored scavenged items: a blue-uniformed toy soldier I'd stolen from my brother, who had an excess of toys but who favoured that one above all others; a red ribbon my mother wore in her hair and which tickled me one night when she came back from dinner and bent over my bed to kiss me; a bird skull from my father's cabinet—a falcon perhaps, though I was never able to ask because I'd stolen it. I kept this odd assortment of treasures wrapped in a cloth behind the links of logs stacked against the wall. One day, reaching for my parcel, my hand glanced something soft and warm. I lit a match and peered around the back of the pile. There was a rather large mouse, brown and still, bleeding on its back where one of the cats might have got it. In the quick fuse of my match's light I saw his whiskers twitch. *Don't touch,* I thought. This was one of the cardinal rules of my childhood—a rule my mother liked to recite in kitchens and shops, on walks through town or in the elegant homes of our relations. *Look* was the other imperative—usually from my father—his finger creating a sightline meant to better me through exposure to animals, ships, modes of industry, work he thought bore some stamp of innovation. I dropped my hand back again behind the woodpile, the rough cut of the logs against my cheek, the smell sweet. I felt for the mouse. He did not skitter when I grabbed him and remained limp in my hand as I pulled him out from behind the wood and onto the dirt floor in front of me. His breath, the rise and fall of his damp brown flank, was slow. I nudged him sideways and placed one finger on the place where I imagined his heart would be. I felt nothing. I thought of Martin then, of his dullness and jaundiced eyes, and wished, stupidly, he could be there with me. 'Maus,' I said, trying to call some aspect of him toward me. 'Maus!' Nothing. The blood beside the claw mark was drying. His back appeared broken. I touched his forehead with one finger and his nose twitched up. *Such small teeth, and yet people are so afraid of you,* I thought. I stroked his face for ten or so minutes, and then I bashed his head in with a log. This made a mess, and I cried because I didn't want to do it—but I didn't know what else to do. I buried him in a shallow hole outside the shed and went in for dinner. I don't know why I'm thinking about that mouse now.

SHORTLY AFTER MY ARRIVAL on the island I had the good fortune to make the acquaintance of a local businessman. He was a quick man in his thirties who dealt in furniture and who frequented the hotel's public house in the evening. His business involved the production of basic and affordable furniture—chairs, tables, sideboards and the like—designed with the local pines in mind and suitable for the island's farming and fishing families, alongside more elaborate pieces, replicas of designs popular on the continent. These latter pieces were made by commission—usually with imported mahogany—in a local workshop where he employed two excellent carpenters. I met this man on the sea road on a gusty day shortly after my arrival. As the gentleman's English was excellent and mine rapidly improving from my practice with the staff at the hotel, we fell to talking. He offered to drive me around the island and over to his business, which he was due to visit that afternoon. I have forgotten his name but can remember his ruddy face, his wide nose, how he laughed with his entire body.

The drive was magnificent. His was one of seven cars on the whole of the island, and save for three riders on horses and a young boy driving a pony cart, we did not pass other human beings. First he took me north, where we trekked into a field that held two very old standing stones; then we drove even farther north to a loch renowned for fishing and the cultivation of oysters. After this we went north again, past low mountains and up to the top of the island where a white towered lighthouse stood in the distance on a rocky promontory. There, he wanted to show me a particularly good view so we started out on a grassy track, first passing a group of wild goats who were nibbling at the knots of seaweed, then setting a host of gulls aloft as we rounded the bend toward the wide expanse of the sea.

By three in the afternoon we were driving south again toward my companion's workshop, the narrow road taking us past a series of white buildings with peaked roofs and smokestacks, which he said housed a local distillery, and then past a charming fishing village where the weekly market was held.

The man's workshop was behind the island's great house, in a series of buildings that also contained a smithy and a tack shop and a new automotive garage. The estate house itself was shuttered, as the owner was frequently on the mainland, though his dogs were wandering about—a pack of four setters minded by one of the senior stable hands. The furniture shop was long and narrow, laid out to ensure ease in production—from the intake of the lumber to the cutting and sizing of the wood, to the woodworking and joinery. Despite having sat on some very fine pieces of furniture in the local hotel, I had not expected to find such master craftwork out here on the edge of the continent.

The two carpenters in the shop appeared to be in their early thirties, near to my own age at the time, but their work and the ease with which they undertook it spoke to more years of experience than they could have had. The taller of the two had scarred hands and an almost impenetrable accent. He was working on the dowels of a beautiful Queen Anne style chair, the back panel of which was inset with a graceful design of grapevines and leaves—a design popular in Florence that year and which these carpenters were replicating based solely on drawings they had received.

I had numerous questions for the carpenters and my host amiably 'translated' their answers. 'How,' I asked, 'does one map a proper design from an illustration?' 'Do you prefer to innovate or stay true to the model and form requested?' 'Is each model intended to be an exact replica—down to the curl of the grape leaf'—this, I had observed, the younger of the carpenters was entrusted with—'or is it preferable to have each chair retain some unique marker that might set it apart?' The carpenters were amused by my questions. They informed me that the chairs they were working on were intended to be indistinguishable from those upon which the drawings were based, the etchings were to be identical; one should not be able to distinguish, if they did their work well, one chair from another. The idea that they would put a motif of their own design, some symbolic signature, into the work amused them; it was an extension of themselves they were disinclined to gift to other people's property. They took a certain amount of pride, I realized, in the completion of a work that would bear no trace of them.

At five, when the sky was getting dark, the younger man's wife brought the men mugs of tea and a thick loaf of bread and a round of soft cheese made from sheep's milk. I was offered some bread and cheese and sat amongst the wood curls and sawdust on a long bench the men had made, observed attentively by one of the laird's large-muzzled bitches who'd wandered in to lie down by the open doorway. This idea of replication was not, I knew, the thing my adviser had told me to look for, not the idea to add to my plodding thoughts on bridges and forms. But the hours I spent in the company of these men conjured in me something of equal value . . . the gift of observing a group of people who seemed to feel at home in their world.

I am not at home in the world now. Even the wine the waiter pours into my glass fails to comfort me. Commissioner Estévez had ordered Spanish wine and its earthiness, its green-stem-like quality reminds me with every sip that I am not in a place I know.

The waiter at the Dorada is one of the few old men I've noticed since we arrived in the village. He's in his late sixties, maybe early seventies, although I am aware that war stresses people in different ways. I think from his deference he is an able survivor: I watch how he moves knives and forks crosswise over the empty plates and lifts the offending platters up and away from our faces with minimal interference, as if he could stand beside you for the duration of a crisis and remain unnoticed.

Gone, amongst the citizens of Portbou, are overt signs of affiliation. It's difficult to tell which side of the civil war people stood on or how they might have survived it. The Republicans—if there are any true Republicans left—have grown quiet. Even back in Marseilles, a city overrun with émigrés and refugees—some of them Spanish—and French soldiers in plain clothes, we could usually surmise who was who. This is the survivor's game: knowing who might give you bread and who might shoot you the second your back is turned. This waiter, with his pressed black jacket, white shirt and polished shoes must have been one of those who sided with the fascists, or who stayed neutral enough that he might as well have sided with them—otherwise, he would not still be here in this restaurant serving these corrupt men; he would not, given his age, be here among the living on this earth.

The plates are cleared and a round of coffee is ordered. Suzanne excuses herself to the lavatory. Señor Porras raises a hand and Alejandro, who has kept one eye on the table for the last hour, is suddenly off his seat at the bar, drifting behind Suzanne and taking up station outside the ladies' restroom. Porras and Noguerra have drunk too much, which tells me that the local Guardia Civil don't have access to black market luxuries to the extent that Estévez does. Estévez, for all of his girth, barely ate anything. The meal was all show: waving and finger-snapping and joking, assessing us and trying to get us drunk.

'So, you must wonder why you're here,' Estévez says, looking Bernard in the eye. He wipes his mouth with a linen napkin and then tosses it toward the centre of the table. 'It's not that your papers are in question, they're very good,' he says. 'It's rather the issue of a new decree from General Franco and a request from our friends to the north that all transit visas from Marseilles be cancelled. Which makes these'—and here he waves his hand over our stack of documents—'useless.' He pauses to smile like a poor salesman. 'Now, of course, Herr Gabler might be helpful here, perhaps securing an exemption from his friends in Berlin, though he is a busy man and such a favour might raise questions. Unless, of course, you can also be of assistance to him.'

I look at Bernard. Why tell us this now, when Suzanne is away from the table? And why address this blackmail to Bernard, with only a few quick cursory glances at me?

'Of course, as teachers, academics, simple artisans—you wouldn't be able to help us much. But as men of intellect, who worked in the great city of Paris, perhaps you can.' He extends his hand toward Herr Gabler, who clicks open a briefcase and lifts out a sheet of paper on which two columns of names are written in black ink. 'The list isn't too long,' Estévez says, 'it won't take you but five minutes. Again, I can make no promises, but perhaps Herr Gabler can—if, of course, you can help us locate some of these individuals?'

I glance down at the paper and when I look up from the scrawled names, Suzanne is back at the table. She is taking everything in—the list of names, my hands on it—as if in her absence some form of agreement has been made. I see now Estévez's thinking—his attempt, at every moment, to divide us, to create the illusion that some sort of collusion might be taking place.

'The border is closed,' I tell Suzanne in French. 'We are now required to have different exit visas from France. This is a list Herr Gabler would like us to look at.'

Suzanne takes her seat slowly.

I push the list back to Gabler. 'I don't know any of these names.'

'But you have not really read the list, professor,' Gabler says.

I force a laugh. 'I'm not a professor, Herr Gabler, though you flatter me with the designation.' But I know it is this word, 'professor,' that seals my fate.

When Gabler calls me professor, it becomes clear to me that our charade is falling apart. This assignation had been omitted on my passport and on all my documents. For Herr Gabler to know I had spent five years teaching, first in Bremen and then in Berlin, meant access to my biography, meant—unless these men were baiting me—that he knew where I was from, what faith I'd been born into, and where my sympathies lay. Throughout dinner, our hosts intimated that they suspected some of our documents were embellished, but it is only when Gabler calls me professor that I

AISLINN HUNTER

understand they know precisely who we are. And I understand that the offer to inform could mean more than safe
passage. If we gave them information about some of the
names on the list, among them Olivier's—the forger of one
of the very documents that sit on the table in front of us—it
might mean our lives.

Herr Gabler's eyes meet mine. I gaze at his long, narrow
face, the grey wells of his eyes, and I wonder what principles
he lives by. I think of the word for criminal in the language
that Gabler and I both spoke as children. I despise him and
I fight to keep that expression to myself. And so, with great
effort, I turn my attention to the table now emptied of
everything but coffee cups and silver spoons, and I feel, in
that moment, incredibly tired.

'I would like to smoke,' I say. Using the table for support, I stand up. When it becomes clear that I have no cigarettes of my own, Señor Porras pulls one from his silver case.
I accept his cigarette and Noguerra, beside me, lights it. 'If
you please,' I say, and I walk toward the door and into the
darkening night, Alejandro falling into place behind me.

Outside, under the snake of La Dorada's bougainvillea,
I inhale and let the cigarette's smoke curl around my mouth,
savouring this old habit. Turning toward the planted palms
so that those inside the restaurant can't see me speaking, I
ask Alejandro, 'Is this typical? Do they always bring émigrés
here and show them lists and ask them questions?'

The guard says nothing. I glance over at him to be sure
he's heard me. Then I shake my head in disdain and exhale

another cloud of smoke. I still have the taste of wine in my mouth, the taste of these very hills above me—the wine served at dinner was a local variety, Grenache perhaps, which the pickers we walked in with might have plucked from these very terraces. When, I wondered, was the last time Alejandro drank wine? I offer him my cigarette but he refuses it.

From where we stand on the carpet of the El Dorado walkway I can see the front of the Paradou patio down the street, the empty table where I sat yesterday, and beyond that the gate that leads to your mother and father's house, Pia, and the square of golden light emanating from the window that looks out over your yard.

'Who lives there?' I ask.

Alejandro follows my gaze to your house on the hillside. 'A businessman. He owns a number of mines in South America.' Alejandro turns toward the bay and in the moonlight I study his strong features, the divot of a scar on his forehead. 'It's not his house,' he says after a minute. 'It belonged to the mayor. He and his family are just staying there.'

And so I picture the man who is your father sitting at the table where the mayor once sat, where I imagine you are sitting now: his clean-shaven face, his combed hair, the cufflinks and polished shoes. I picture him making excuses for who he is dealing with and for the questions he already knows the answers to, but would never ask. I picture him as he was yesterday when he passed by the Paradou: such cleanliness, such precision—and I recall with difficulty the daily vanity with which I must once have attended to my own appearance in a vanished world . . . the hair comb, the razor, the boar bristle brush I used on the shoulders of my good suit.

There was one name on Herr Gabler's list that I recognized immediately: Gaston. Gaston, who would be guilty of what? He is a pacifist, a socialist, a philosopher. He has written anti-fascist articles for French magazines and journals but he is mostly a man who keeps his head in books. The last time I saw him he was trying to help two of our mutual Jewish friends secure safe-conduct passes so that they could leave France. That his name is on the list, that he's not been struck off, as a handful of names were, gives me hope, even if the hope is for him and the work he is doing and not for me.

The cigarette I'm smoking, hand-rolled from good tobacco, is sweet. Something I could get used to if afforded the chance. I watch its embers brighten against the dark night and the quiet street. When I finish it, I turn reluctantly to go in.

'Only once before,' Alejandro says, hesitantly. 'A week ago. A group of four, the same table. One of the men gave information on two of the names and he was taken back to the station and let go. The others, and the two children who were travelling with them, were escorted back across the border the next morning.'

I WORKED ON TWO ESSAYS while I was on your island, Pia: one on replication, using the chairs in the workshop as a starting point for my investigation, and a second essay on the use and placement of mirrors. That was when I began to think about Narcissus.

It was my habit back then to begin any essay by outlining my investigations in fragments, in case I came across some additional fact or addendum to my argument midway through my first attempt at a thesis. Gaston once chided me for this, saying that it demonstrated a lack of conviction, but I felt that it gave me a wider berth . . . that even as I searched for ideas to support my thinking I was simultaneously searching for contradictions.

The idea for the mirror essay came to me while I was staying in the hotel on the promontory. It had rained for three days straight—a relentless downpour unlike any I'd encountered before—and so I'd stayed in, taking my notebook first to the guest lounge, then to the bar where I took my meals, and then back to my small room each evening. It was while making this circuit that I realized there was only one mirror in the whole establishment—an ornate oval one on the first-floor stairwell landing, a mirror that caused me to meet myself on the steps before descending to the main floor. The first time I noticed it, I was reminded of how, when we were children, my mother liked to tell my sister Meira and me about all manner of mythical creatures: humans enchanted into animal forms, wailing women who presaged death, bulls with crooked horns who were prizes from the gods. These stories had come to her through her father's side of the family, and were largely enlisted by her as a means of ensuring our best behaviour lest we sneak down to the kitchen for cake after bedtime or touch things that did not belong to us. One night when I was eight or so, I was allowed into my mother's room to help her get ready for dinner at a neighbour's house. I was assigned the task of bringing her the velvet tray that held her rings. I remember how she sat in front of her mirror, the skirt of her mauve dress spilling over the side of the chair, so that I had to walk carefully around it to approach her with the selection.

'Have I told you about the taise?' she asked.

'No,' I said, although I didn't know for certain—my 'no' was meant to encourage her story.

'Well,' she began, daubing a brush flecked with fine white powder onto her forehead and face, 'the taise is a ghost . . . but not just any ghost—your *own* ghost.' She looked at me through the mirror. 'Imagine,' she continued, 'that you're walking in the woods of our property and between the trees you see someone, but you can't quite see who it is. So you walk closer. Maybe you even call out, "Hello, who's there?"— but no answer. What then?' she asks.

'I come home.'

She opened her drawer, placed the brush inside, and then turned to the mirror again with a cloth that she patted over her face to make the white powder less stark. 'But what if you recognize something about the figure? Would you go toward it?' Her eyebrows in the mirror shot up.

I thought about her question—about my real answer, and about what I imagined she might wish me to say. 'Yes,' I said eventually, though my voice sounded uncertain.

She placed the cloth in the drawer and closed it. 'And what if, when you moved through the trees and came to the figure'—and here she shifted on her chair to face me—'you saw that the figure was you?'

I searched her face—her green eyes narrowed playfully, her mouth suppressing a smile. She had arranged her brown hair in a twist so that her neck appeared long and elegant. I wanted to push my face into the crook of it, place my cheek against the pulse where a blue vein ran down to her heart from behind her earlobe.

'What then, my pet?' Her expression turned serious.

'I'd run,' I said.

'That's right,' she replied, placing her hands around the sides of my arms and gripping me uncomfortably. 'You'd run.'

I reminded my mother of this conversation some five or six years later before I left home for boarding school. We were in the sitting room and she was making a bird mask for a costume party. There was a spray of loose feathers at her feet and one of the cats was batting at them—a grey cat with amber eyes whose twin had died the winter before. 'What was it called?' I asked. 'That doppelgänger you terrified me with when I was young?'

'The taise?' She lifted her needle up through the black velvet ribbon that would hold the mask in place, then threaded it down again.

'Did you mean to terrify me so?'

'Yes, I think I did.' She glanced up at me and then went back to the ribbon. 'Do you remember my father? Your grandfather? He had white hair, hardly spoke a word of German, and smelled like pipe smoke. He had a silver watch and chain that you were obsessed with that one time he came to visit.' I assembled the attributes she mentioned in my mind but came up with nothing—only floating images and a tang of failure at not being able to remember someone who had once moved so intimately through my mother's life.

'Well, one day he was up on a ladder fixing a hole in the thatch roof and he turned and saw someone standing at the edge of his field by the property line. The figure called for help, waving his arms.' My mother smiled and smoothed her already crisp skirt. 'And my father, half on the ladder and half up on the thatch, shouted back at him, "What's the matter? What's wrong?" My mother, hearing the shouting, came out and asked my father, "Whatever in the world are you going on about?"'

I laughed without meaning to; I always enjoyed my mother's imitations of her parents' different accents.

'And my father pointed to the figure by the edge of the field and said, "That man there, he's calling for help." "What man?" my mother snapped, because even standing on an upturned bucket she couldn't see what he was seeing. "Yonder," my father said, and he stood up and pointed, "a man as tall as me, as—" and then he lost his footing and fell off the roof . . . and I was suddenly without a father.'

———

When I re-enter La Dorada after my cigarette, I walk toward the table with new energy. Until now I'd been trying to imitate Bernard's nonchalance and Suzanne's pleasantries but my efforts have felt forced. Herr Gabler has been observing me throughout the meal, occasionally engaging with Señor Porras, and two or three times directing a question toward Suzanne or Bernard—but always watching me to see how I react to what he asks and how they respond.

I have a sense of Herr Gabler's story. He's a type, the way we are all becoming types. Born along the outskirts of some city, or in some burgeoning provincial town, an outsider caught up in a movement that promises him that he and his country can be something important, monumental. As if the country was nothing before—the lakes flush with fish, the forests rich with trees and the people making their honest living. Gabler would have aspired to some trade or vocation at an early age and failed at it—his parents not believing in him, or believing too much. The school and his teachers would have told him his efforts and skills were unacceptable. And so the day would arrive when, standing in the gravel yard amongst his fellow students, or sitting at a café with friends who have caught him in a lie about his doings, he is humiliated and shamed. If he is young, this might come with a beating. If he is older, ostracizing him will be punishment enough. Either way, the world turns its shoulder to him. Under normal conditions he would go off, live quietly, imagine some way to make the world turn back in adulation. But perhaps in this world we inhabit now,

Herr Gabler's shame occurred as the curriculum changed, as Jewish teachers were fired and Jewish students expelled, and decoding the facial attributes of Jews became a test. Perhaps he ceased to be seen as a failure, a problem. Instead, he acquired a uniform and a gun, stayed quiet, dug when told to dig, and marched someone off when the signal was given. Perhaps Herr Gabler's compliance allowed him to gain access to a car when everyone within 150 kilometres of him was walking between towns with no access to petrol and no relationship to local power. Perhaps his subservience became a kind of rank and he rose. Now, in private he rations but in public he eats large, expensive meals so that others can witness his excess. How he studied the second spoon this evening, trying to discern what to do with it! I almost said something then, and am glad I did not.

But perhaps this is not Herr Gabler's story, and his truth is something outside the limits of what I can imagine— though there is no narrative in which I can see him standing for what is just or good. He will view me through a similar lens: a boche, émigré, refugee, apatride subject to Article 19. I watch him now as I walk back to the table—smug and pale—and I want, with everything I have, maybe even my life, to spit in his face. But I'm tired, and I find it increasingly difficult to measure the value of such an act.

In Marseille, when we lined up for two days outside the consulate for our Spanish transit visas, we were so exhausted by the time we reached the front of the queue that we couldn't differentiate between those forming the human chain of misery alongside us and those who were causing it. This is why it's called la pagaille—the great turmoil. There are times when we see straight, and there are times when we heave and sigh together only to rush apart at the sound of boots on the ground.

I pull my chair out from the table and take my seat, observing Bernard's tensed shoulders, Suzanne's flushed face. Herr Gabler has placed the list on the table again and Bernard is staring at it as if it's a dead thing. These men are done with their our-hands-are-tied apologies, their limp excuses about the need for exit visas and new directives.

'If you don't cooperate, you will be escorted back to the border and handed over to the police,' Herr Gabler says. He angles his head at me and adds, 'And you will be sent back, under custody, to Germany.'

'But a wonderful meal, non?' says the commissioner. He pats Suzanne on her shoulder with a fat hand and stands up. 'And this?' He indicates the sheet of names. 'Charity.'

Señor Porras and Señor Noguerra stand too, and Herr Gabler picks his cap off a low stool beside him. 'We're giving you the night to think,' he says.

The commissioner surveys the restaurant, which is starting to fill up for dinner. 'Where's your carabinero, Porras?'

Porras raises his hand and Alejandro wends his way through the tables until he is again beside us.

'Good man,' the commissioner says. I notice that none of them consider that Alejandro has had no time for a proper rest; none of them thinks to order someone to relieve him.

'Now, listen,' the commissioner says, 'if they make a run for it in the night you have my permission to shoot them.' He smiles widely as if he's just made a joke and nods at each one of us. Then he lifts the list of names from the table and tips it into my hands. 'Sleep well.'

Suzanne, Bernard and I walk back to the hotel under a dark sky, the sea indistinguishable from the hulking silhouettes of the bluffs. As we walk I pay attention to the feel of the world on my skin: the evening air along the back of my neck, above my shirt collar; how the saline smell of the sea lilts with the drop in temperature . . . now a drift of brine, now nothing, pure air. Bernard is walking ahead with purpose. Alejandro lets him go. He knows by now that we will not act for ourselves, that we are in this together, as far as together can take us.

Behind me is the gate to your parents' home, where your mother is maybe, just now, tucking you into bed, Pia—your mother who will survive this year and the next and who will forge a way through this interval. Do people still tell their children bedtime stories in this age? Tales set in bristling woods? A man on a roof who sees himself in someone else and calls out? Dumb animals suddenly gifted with speech? A look over the shoulder that turns the loved one to ash? What need is there to scare children— the world is enough.

We round the corner to the hotel and see that the lights outside the entrance and on the main floor have been turned off. Electricity is still being rationed. Upstairs on the second floor, however, the room next to mine—unoccupied since our arrival—appears to be lit by a globe light or lantern. Suzanne, walking beside me, looks up at the second floor, takes my hand and squeezes it. I don't know why, but this brings tears to my eyes—the gentle hopefulness of it when I feel no hope at all.

The hotel lobby is navigable in the moonlight. The white curtains have been pushed back to the view of the sea that would once have made this place a draw for those driving along the coast or taking the train south to Barcelona. Alejandro stops at the foot of the stairs and informs us that he will allow us to meet in Bernard and Suzanne's room to discuss the paper. 'Una hora,' he says, holding a single finger up. He has feigned a stern expression—a young man trying to swim toward authority from the far side of exhaustion. If the lobby were warmer, if he had a light blanket, he might fall asleep, and Bernard and Suzanne might be able to sneak past him and head into the foothills and back over the col. Or maybe, if he dozes, we can catch him off guard, hit him over the head with something—though his pistol would likely make the outcome unfavourable. To my own surprise, I have automatically taken an inventory of the hotel—the large ceramic lamp, the heavy phone on the reception desk, the swinging doors that lead to a kitchen where there will be a drawer of knives. 'Ràpidament,' Alejandro snaps, and we trudge up the stairs, past the door with the sliver of light slipping out.

Once in her room, Suzanne slips off her shoes and sits on the bed, one hand on either side of her hips.

'Did they hurt you before we arrived?' Bernard asks. He moves toward the balcony to see if anyone is watching the hotel.

'No,' Suzanne says. 'It was all just,' she pauses, breathes out. 'They aren't making it up. It isn't us, this isn't just *for us*, there's been a new mandate about visas from Marseilles. It went into effect yesterday, as we were told. I think they're just taking advantage of it.'

Bernard laces his palms together behind his head. 'A bribe?' he asks. 'What about the guard? How much can we afford?'

I shake my head. Alejandro would not be spared if we escaped.

I pull Gabler's list out, and smooth it onto the desk. We survey the names. If we could get this list out, back to France, those whose names are cited could be warned, and people would know not to try for the border. Bernard runs his finger down the page, his hand shaking.

'I think I'm going to be sick,' Suzanne says, slowly getting up and moving toward the door.

'Here,' Bernard hands her the ceramic basin and sits her back down on the bed. 'Wine or meat or something else?'

'Meat, I think. It was so rich.'

Amongst us we know a handful of names—Gaston's, Olivier the forger's, and a couple named Julien and Klara who Bernard and I had hid with two months ago at a farmhouse near Gien.

'Look—' Bernard points to the name Bernadette Gosse. It's misspelled and in a cramped handwriting, so he'd missed it at first. She is one of Artun's other clients—a sculptor who'd stayed behind in Paris because she had a new baby and her Czech husband was still in the camp for foreign nationals. 'Why her?' he asks.

Suzanne shakes her head. 'Her baby's only, what, maybe eight months old now?'

This is something I prefer not to think about: trying to survive the war in order to save your children, or giving up your children so you can survive. For months now, it's been rare to see anyone under ten on the city streets or in the villages. After we left Paris, Bernard and I stayed briefly in a house of an acquaintance in the country near Saint Vrain. The Germans were already strafing the fields by then, and walking amongst the refugees, watching the French soldiers hobble home. At night we often passed by a goat shed that I knew held two children. If we found or managed to purchase food, Bernard would take some of it to these children on our way back to the house where we were staying. He'd deke off the road, then rejoin me and say 'the same,' which meant they were still there: an older boy and his younger sister who was sick, and no one sure what medication would be useful. Bernard tried in the days before we left the area to find a doctor willing to come to the village with the medicine most likely to help. But there were no doctors, not even a veterinarian.

'I need to rest,' I say. I wave to Bernard and Suzanne. 'I'll come back in a bit, I just need to close my eyes.'

'Of course,' Suzanne says.

Bernard places his hand on my arm and squeezes it.

I walk out to the hall and pause outside the door with the slant of light under it. But what good can a stranger do? Even if the stranger is good.

My room seems untouched. I check my briefcase for my manuscript; I check my notes on the side table, my money tucked into a hole I made in the spare pillow in the closet. I sit on the bed someone has gone through the motions of making. We still do not have our papers but it wouldn't be impossible in Marseilles to get such papers again. Unlikely—but not impossible.

I'm glad not to have had children, though it would be dishonest to attribute that sentiment to the state of the world around me. I was always too selfish, and truthfully, I found children tiresome even when I was a child myself—couldn't even pretend with my little cousins that their shrieks of joy at some bright present amused me. Once, in the gap between the wars, when Meira and I were both staying at her house in Berlin, she turned on me mid-conversation, perceiving some slight in a comment I'd made about her and Franz's struggle to bear children. A better brother would have remembered what he'd said, but my comment had immediately gone out of my head. I remember standing on the ornate rug in the entry of her home, hat on, gloves in hand, ready to head over to the university, wishing—while she railed at me—that she'd give me some indication of what I'd said. She refused. I think what I wanted then was not to soothe her, not to be forgiven, but to be able to assess whether it was she or I who was in the wrong. By the time I returned for dinner, she had fumed through my seven hours in class and at the library, fumed through Kant and Hegel and Horkheimer. Franz was late again, and though I sensed that the empty place at the head of the table annoyed her more than I did, I took the brunt of the anger. That's when she said the thing she thought would hurt me most: 'It's your unborn child who's lucky.' Her chin quivered. 'To have you as a father? I can't imagine the disappointment.'

If I had a son, he'd likely be Alejandro's age. This softens me to Alejandro, but not sentimentally, only factually—a way, when other means have failed, to imagine some kinship between us. But I know that kinship is a cousin to fidelity: it is how we attach to others, to those whose countenance we bear, whose history informs us, whose view from the balcony mirrors our own. My father's decisions, his travels and stories; my mother's affirmations and her strangeness, her willingness to live in a country she was not born in—all of these have helped to bring me here, to this room in a hotel in Portbou. Why would I inflict my choices on a child, when the past, when the books and ideas that fill my present, have been everything? All these cries about the future! Until yesterday—until you, Pia—I could not even glimpse its trajectory.

What could I write to explain these hours and days? Pia, you are like a dream one has, a harbinger. Like the box where I placed all the treasures of my childhood, except that my treasures now are merely things I've seen, and ideas, and strings of words. Still, I am placing them all in you.

*M*orning light slants through the storm's heavy clouds. On the stretch of grass between the hotel patio and the thin wire fence of the promontory, two men in oilskin coats stand in the pelting rain looking through binoculars toward the sea. The taller of the two clasps his cap onto his head in the wind, his heavy coat flaps lifting.

Pia's room is cold, so she shrugs on a sweater—the only one she has, purchased this past spring after the barman drove her to the crofter's shop, insisting she buy something to keep herself warm.

The hotel sits above a large bay open to the ocean. Even when the days are mild, the wind crawls under a loose jacket, brings a chill. The village was built 150 years ago. When Pia thumbed through old photos at the local museum she could see how much of the bluff has eroded since then. Otherwise, the buildings are the same: rows of white stone houses with turn-of-the-century terraced archways, windows facing both the street and the horizon. Like every building in the chain along the ridge, the hotel now sits only a hundred metres from the cliff face.

At her window, Pia watches as the men turn from the bluff toward the parking lot, one of them shouting to be heard above the wind.

The builder is in the entryway putting on his coat when Pia steps off the stair landing into the hotel lobby. She'd expected him to come up to her room last night, but had fallen asleep almost as soon as she'd slipped under the covers— and in the morning, she'd woken up alone. He steps forward and says, 'There's wreckage on the beach.' He repeats what has been relayed to him: A boat has gone down. Parts of it are washing up in the bay.

Access to the bay below the hotel is past a 'do not cross' sign a short distance along the coast, where a trail to the beach zigzags through knee-high grasses and over the shelf of rocks that skirts the cliff. In the summer Pia would sometimes go down and sit on the sand with a book. It was usually quiet because the bay isn't safe for swimming.

The builder says he's heading down to the shore, and Pia says, 'I'll come.' He glances at her as if to ask, *Why?* A feeling flares in her chest, similar to the one she'd often experienced after first moving to the island—a response to the quick glances from locals that registered her as a foreigner; and to the middle-aged woman at the corner shop who treated her coldly even after Pia had been buying supplies there for weeks.

'You'll need a good coat,' the builder says. And he walks out the door.

Pia finds the prep cook's coat again, still in the kitchen office, and borrows it. She pulls on her waterproof boots.

From the top of the trail she counts six people—including the builder—hauling up debris from the shore. A dozen wood slats have washed onto the sand along with a large beam and its rigging. One of the men is carrying a bundle of fishing net. A dog—one of the island's working breeds—trots along at his heels. Beyond the beach, the sea is heaving, and when it wells, slats of wood sometimes appear in the froth.

The descent to the beach is tricky and Pia has to watch her feet. The long grass is blowing sideways and the rain makes everything slick. In the early summer she'd run down this trail, but now every step feels treacherous. It was in the summer—when Pia had been on the island only a month—that she thought she saw a fox. She'd been halfway down the slope with a book under her arm and a canister of tea in her hand. The fox appeared in the format of a flare of russet and the flick of a tail coursing through the stonecrop and spurrey before veering up the bank and over the grassy ledge. When Pia later told the barman what she'd seen, he had balked. There was a fox farm on the island a few decades ago, he told her, but a couple of the foxes had escaped their pens and killed some lambs, so they'd all been shot.

'A dog,' he said. 'That's what you saw.'

But Pia knew better. Dogs on the island weren't that shade of red.

When she reaches the skirt of dark stone that marks the final drop to the beach, Pia stops. She recognizes everyone gathered here: the builder, the gentleman farmer she sometimes sees heading toward the fields with his herding dog, the widow's son, the woman who works part-time at the post office, a local fisherman who's in the bar every night at nine, and another local who brings his wife to the restaurant on special occasions . . . the two of them dressed up and enjoying the candlelight and black-tie servers. Seeing Pia, the dog trots toward her along the shoreline, his barks dragged off by the wind. Pia looks up at the wild sky. For the first time since she's lived here, there are no birds to be seen.

ONCE IN THE LATE SPRING, before the tourists arrived, the prep cook had taken Pia out on his motorcycle to show her the remote parts of the island. He'd been on the island for a year longer than she had been, but every time Pia asked him a question about the place, he'd shrug and say, 'I have no idea.' Midway through the ride they'd stopped to sit on the side of the road near an expanse of bog. The prep cook smoked and birds lifted up and flew down, flitting around them. Pia asked, 'What's this? What's that?' He couldn't name a single thing. She put her hand around a clump of bushy-tipped grass and raised her eyebrows.

'Grass,' he'd said, and shrugged.

She pointed to a bird with a yellow beak who was staring at them from a nearby rock, eyes dark as nail heads.

'Christ if I know.'

'Some tour,' Pia joked.

He stubbed out his cigarette and stood up. 'Come on,' he said, 'let me show you a shipwreck.'

The so-called wreck was more like the bones of a ship, or like the jaw of an animal coming up through the sand. Up close, its rusted frame was slick with moss and seaweed. There was a thick chain along one of the girders and both it and the bolt holes on the nearby crossbeam had seaweed strung through their cavities. Pia knew a few of the local seaweeds from some of the chef's dishes—but those were fresh and green or purple, and the seaweed banding the ship's frame was brown and stringy. It made the wreck look as if it had feathers.

The prep cook had brought along a camera and now he lifted it to his face. It was a bulky black and silver thing that he spent a lot of time adjusting. It occurred to Pia that maybe he was one of those people who could only see the world through mediums other than his own eyes. She asked what he was going to do with his photographs of the boat. 'I just like the shapes,' he explained, 'how things can became abstracted into another form, but also how abstracted forms can cohere into *something*.' His face, when he said this, relaxed into an expression of hopeful vulnerability, and Pia had felt a flash of tenderness toward him.

ON THE BEACH, THE TWO MEN with the best raingear stand near the tideline. They step into the lather when slats of wood or sections of rigging come toward the shore. Pia and the postmistress—a blonde woman of Pia's age, broad-shouldered and strong—drag the planks up the beach and put them in a pile. Pia has forgotten her gloves, and in between retrieving planks she rubs her hands together or bunches them under her sweater. The water is cold and the wind stings.

The builder is out on the bluff with binoculars, scanning for survivors. One of the island's biggest trawlers is due up from the south port to help with the search, but the port is thirty minutes away, and the sea past the rocks is still heaving. Among those gathered on the shore, there's a sense of purpose: the widow's son is relaying information to the hotel clerk, who's on the radio back at the hotel; the fisherman is calmly inspecting the rigging and buoyed netting as it washes up. Pia has a sense that this has happened before—that the islanders know how the coming hours will unfold. Only the builder seems visibly upset. When, earlier, he'd rushed out of the hotel so quickly, Pia had suddenly thought: *That isn't the builder going down to the beach; it's the doctor.*

There's nothing else to drag up the beach, so Pia sits on a rock to rest. What had she expected to see? A ship listing in the bay? A gutted hull? Lifeboats? She remembers the last time she had a similar sensation—of turning a corner into an event that had already happened, when you expected something to be happening. It was, then, the difference between one breath and the next: *I'm walking down the dim hall (I have a mother), I'm turning into the dank room the man has indicated (I have a mother), I look to where he points along the far side of the wall.*

THE BUILDER SPOTS THE FIRST LIFEJACKET, on the skirt of low rocks on the west side of the bay. The waves are too high for anyone to retrieve it, and soon Pia goes back to pulling wood planks out of the waves. Some of the planks have peeling blue paint on one side. There's a bar of white pigment on another plank, thick like the stem of a letter. A moment later, another net comes bobbing in.

As the rain eases up, the hotel clerk appears, wending her way down to the beach under an umbrella that dips sideways whenever she loses her footing.

'It's not one of ours,' she says, when the group has assembled. 'Everyone's accounted for.' So far there's nothing to name the ship, no reports of missing vessels on the radio. The distress call had been a voice blanketed by static.

The fisherman pushes back the hood on his jacket and squints at the scudded clouds. The lines around his eyes and mouth place him in his sixties—although Pia knows that island life can age people. 'How far out is the trawler?' he asks.

'Should be here any time,' the clerk says.

Pia looks out toward the frothing waves. On the far side of the bay, just in her line of sight, the dog digs at something in the sand.

An hour later, Pia jogs up to the hotel to get tea and sandwiches for the group on the beach. As she hangs the prep cook's dripping coat on the peg inside the door, she overhears the bride's father asking about the ferry. There's the honeymoon flight from the mainland, he says, his wife's appointment with a specialist, the unexpected cost of another night's rooms. The hotel owner's brother, who has come in to relieve the desk clerk, scratches his head and says, 'They might run tomorrow. Depends on whether or not there's damage to the port.'

Most of the wedding party has gathered in the bar, where the staff is providing soup and salad. Light banter fills the room—Pia can hear the bride in a nearby booth, recounting a story that makes her bridesmaids laugh, little notes of pleasure bright as glass.

The main kitchen is dark and quiet. Pia puts the kettle on and slices bread for a dozen sandwiches. She checks the temperature in the fridge, which is chugging along on half-power, and pulls out the cheese and meat she'd put under ice yesterday. Then she rummages in a crate for crisp lettuce. There'll be no deliveries today, no restaurant service. The road between the hotel's suppliers and the hotel—a rutted single track that cuts across the island's midriff before dipping into a vale—is flooded; the phone lines are down. The chef isn't a local but he's been on the island five years, would understand the way a storm shifts priorities: livestock that need tending, damaged roofs.

In the two wars that framed Pia's childhood, people often went without. In the village by the sea there were food shortages and power outages. The fascia of the church—the calm faces and supplicating hands of the saints—were left to boulder the ground. Every Sunday, Pia's neighbour, a woman in a grey coat and black square heels who was mother to four children under eight, took the wafer onto her tongue like a fledgling. Every week she became thinner.

The oldest son of this woman was one of Pia's only friends. The family lived in a two-storey house opposite the foot of the hill where Pia's family lived. The boy was big-boned with a wide, easy smile and a loud staccato laugh. If Pia asked him a question—*What games do you like? How many hens do you have?*—he wouldn't answer. But he was good at running and drawing, and once they became friends he'd greet Pia by raising both hands over his head and shouting her name.

It was around this time that Pia's father started taking her on regular morning walks. He said it was good to be out in the fresh air, but Pia sensed the walk was a demand of her mother's: that her father get her out of the house, be more present in his daughter's life. One day they climbed higher than usual, north from the village. After an hour or so, they came to a spot he seemed to recognize. 'I want to tell you something,' he said. They rounded a bend high above sea level and he pointed toward a dusty trail. 'Thousands of people had to leave the country along that path.' To their right, on the slope of the hill, the shell of a burned-out car rested against a rock, grass and weeds growing out of it, a gaping hole where a canvas roof had been. Two tires, which had rolled further down the slope, lay a short distance away on top of sprouting wildflowers. He tried to explain the civil war, saying, 'I want you to remember more about this place than your silly dolls and your dress-up games and books.' He gestured toward the ridge. 'People are buried there, Pia. In shallow graves with no markers. Your new friend? His father is buried there too.'

Pia remembers studying the scrub that grew over the unmarked graves her father had indicated. She took in the flicking heads of the marigolds and waited, as when her father said prayers at dinner, for a signal that the solemn moment had passed. She hadn't understood—graves did not look like this, and the traffic of human history, its misery had never been her concern . . . so a part of her dismissed what he'd said, even as another part stored the memory. Eventually he lit a cigarette and they started back down the mountain, the crickets chirring in the grass, a lizard skittering across the path between them.

PIA WORKS HER WAY back down the trail to the beach. The rain has now turned to drizzle—a light spray, as if the wind is lifting a thin skein of water off the surf. There are fewer whitecaps coming into the bay, less rolling thunder, though farther out on the water the waves are still sizable—washing up against the prow of the trawler that is moving slowly past the bluff. The gulls are back circling the bay and shrugging around the flotsam that's washed up on the sand.

The dog trots over to Pia when she steps off the rocks, soaking wet and happy in his greeting. He sniffs the base of the box she's carrying and then ambles back to the farmer, casting a look over his shoulder to be sure she's following along with the food. More debris has been dragged up toward the cliff face: another dozen planks of wood, an oar, six life vests, a clump of waterlogged clothes that makes Pia picture a suitcase being blown open in a storm. But when she walks closer to the mound, she sees how ragged the clothes are and it occurs to her that these things were probably torn off the bodies they belonged to, in the churning water. A grey sweater; a blue blouse torn at the shoulder; a pair of navy trousers that would fit a child.

Pia turns away and takes the box of sandwiches, the canister of tea and its cups, over to the group who've gathered near the cliff face. The barman has come down from the hotel with a map of the coast, and he and the fisherman are consulting about the tides. There are a few bays north and south along the coastline where something that might help to identify the ship could wash up. Everyone finishes their sandwiches, stacking the teacups back in the box politely, delicately. The postmistress yawns. Even the dog is flagging: he flops down in the windbreak the stack of wood planks has made, his head between his paws. Pia picks up the box and turns toward the foot of the trail; the gulls along the tide line squawk loudly as she approaches. The builder—his face pinched with cold—trudges up from the shore. There are traces of salt around his eyes and mouth from the hour he's spent on the point.

'They've asked me to drive up the coast to look for—' He scrunches his nose and doesn't finish the sentence.

Pia shifts the box so that it rests against her hip. 'I'll come with you.'

The builder's car is parked at his cottage and so he walks over to get it while Pia returns to the hotel and changes into dry clothes. They've been asked to head north on the coast road, to stop at the larger bays and report back if they find anything. This is the part of the island Pia knows best—the direction she chooses every morning when she runs—fields alternating with bog, the shaggy sheep, a few isolated farmhouses before the island's western shoulder. She already knows exactly where the beach accesses are, how the northernmost tip of the island tapers like a finger to the sea.

While she's waiting for the builder Pia finds an extra pair of socks and the gloves she'd forgotten earlier. She stuffs them into a bag. She towel-dries her hair again, quick, brusque movements because her head still feels cold. Then she sits on her bed; breathes.

On top of the dresser is the book she's been reading. It's slight but she doesn't find it easy to understand: the ideas jump around as if the author isn't certain of what he's trying to say. Pia picks it up and opens its torn blue cover, thumbs through its pages. She only has a short chapter to go and then she'll be done with mirrors, can close her eyes and choose another book from the widow's library.

In the section Pia is reading the author is querying what it means to see the world through a mirror, to reveal the world in reverse. He describes at length a fifteenth-century painting of a wealthy couple. They are dressed in velvet coats with ermine trim, and are standing on the plain floorboards of a modest home, a grey-brown dog between them. The work is likely a commission: the commemoration of a betrothal or a marriage. 'Already, in their postures,' the writer says, 'in the man's sombre expression and the woman's downcast gaze, in the slip of her upturned palm, there's a sense of their future. The painting, and their fate, seems fixed . . . but behind the couple is a mirror—a luxury in this time period. This one has been made by glassblowers pouring a metal mixture into a glass sphere, which results in a curved shape that expands the viewer's field of vision. The mirror in the painting shows us the room in reverse and in its full scope: the backs of the couple, the ceiling's beams, the adjacent window, the crowd we did not know about, but who all the while were standing before them.'

'Time,' the philosopher writes, 'is also like this. We know what we know by what's revealed in reflection. These revelations permit us to see the larger world, to better understand what's happened, and to guess at what's to come.'

A knock on the door startles Pia. She sets the book down just as the builder says her name, his voice muffled by the wall between them. And though she could spring up to the door—open it with one easy step forward—she stays on the edge of the bed for a few more seconds, waiting for him to call her name again.

THE SHRIEKING GULLS lead them around the rock bed. The stench is immediate. Pia puts her hand over her nose, almost slips on the slick stone. The smell of the dead seal is blubber-fat and fetid, the animal's entrails welling onto the stony ledge. Overhead the birds turn tight circles, then drop down close to where Pia and the builder stand. The bravest ones perch on the nearby rock face, spreading and flapping their wings.

The tide is retreating, and above the swash the first beach is clear, except for eelgrass and the stranded crabs the birds pick through. Back in the car, the builder wipes the inside of the windshield free of condensation—an old car, a leak he needs to get fixed. He starts the engine, turns onto the road. The sky outside the windshield is a veiled grey: curtains of rain receding in the distance. They drive in silence, the bog to Pia's right brown and still, though every now and again between the coast and the bog a bed of fern crops up—so green it makes Pia think of her abuela's herb garden—the virescent shock of the coriander, parsley and basil in the dull brown planters she tended in the corner of the courtyard. When Pia moved back to her abuela's city at the age of ten, her abuela taught her to cook with those herbs. One of her mother's favourite meals was thyme soup with parsley, and Pia would make this soup when her mother flew back from faraway assignments.

In one of those assignments, Pia's mother covered a students' strike—and in the recording Pia has of that broadcast, her mother describes the crowd, recites the slogans the students have painted on their signs. In another recording,

Pia's mother covers a mining disaster, and in another, an attempted coup. The silence of the bog—this island's quiet as Pia and the builder drive along—feels a hundred years away from that world, a hundred years removed from her mother's witnessing of these events and tipping them into another language so that listeners outside the country— people standing in kitchens, or dressing for work in their bright bedrooms, or driving their cars—could follow the concerns she was reporting, calamities occurring in some 'remote' corner of the world.

Sometimes in the background of the recordings, the rabble of a crowd can be heard, or the blare of traffic, or gusting wind, and these clues ground Pia in the places where her mother once stood. 'The polls are closing,' her mother says, over the protester's chants, 'demonstrations have broken out . . .' '. . . the buildings at the north end of the city have been flattened. Emergency services are having difficulty navigating . . . aftershocks have been reported throughout the region.' In this last one, there's the sound of heavy machinery, and Pia imagines her mother standing near a crane that is clawing at the rubble around her.

When Pia was in her thirties, she received these record- ings as part of her abuela's estate. At the time, Pia was work- ing in a big hotel kitchen that had become renowned. She was an assistant, working morning shifts with a chef de partie who liked to listen to the news at his station. Watching him work, she had seen what it would be like to be some- one with daily rituals: *Now I am kneading the dough, now I am slicing the apples, now, at eleven, I am taking my smoke break in the alley* . . . The rituals were a comfort, a pattern she was happy to slip into, but it always struck her as disquieting—how the dollop of mousse, the fine grating of cinnamon were set against the cacophony of news from far corners of the world.

In Pia's favourite recording, her mother is covering the funeral of a poet who had won a major prize for his work. She praises the poet in a language the poet did not write in. 'Thousands of people are lining the street, crying and throwing flowers as the coffin moves slowly down the road . . .' Then, at the end of the broadcast, she reads one of his poems in his own tongue—in the language she and the poet shared—full of intimations and rhythms that are like the lullabies of Pia's childhood: like the must and rosewood smell of her abuela's armoire, like the gentle thump of her father's briefcase set at the foot of the stairwell when he arrived home.

The builder asks Pia a question, turning in the driver's seat to face her. The bog has become forest now, and Pia inhales the scent of wet pine. How long has she been daydreaming? She shakes her head, as if she's clearing water from her ears, and waits for the builder to ask again. She wants to answer in her own language, to say exactly what she's thinking. His mouth moves, and she tries to concentrate, to hear him over the voice of her mother saying, 'There are troops gathered outside the cemetery . . .' 'These arrests come at a time when . . .' 'Today I am standing in the middle of the plaza . . .'

The stag comes out of nowhere—a blur of rust in front of the windshield, his antlers like knifepoints against the sky.

The builder veers right and the car jolts to a stop a few metres from a stone fence. Pia's head thunks against the side window, but she isn't sure if she is hearing the side of her head hitting the glass or the car clipping the stag's haunch. Then stillness, and a high-pitched hum that must be coming from somewhere inside her. Pia shakes her head and scans the tree line for the animal. He's gone. The builder leans over, turns her face toward his. 'Are you okay?' he asks. He moves his fingers through her hair until she flinches and says, 'Ouch.'

They get out of the car to check for damage, and a group of red deer standing along the hem of woods watch, blinking. After a minute the herd turns away, heads dropping back down to the wet grass.

BEFORE RETURNING TO THE HOTEL, Pia and the builder drive on, and stop at a second bay. The builder leaves Pia in the car. He's gone less than ten minutes, and when he comes back he is winded. 'There's nothing,' he says. On the drive back he asks if she feels light-headed or woozy. He reaches over and touches the sore spot on Pia's head, says, 'You're going to have quite the bump.'

'What kind of doctor were you?' Pia asks. They're moving south through a part of the island that's usually so thick with grazing flocks of sheep that people can spend twenty or thirty minutes on the trackway, their cars inching forward while the sheep, picking through the tufted grass that springs up on both sides of the road, obstinately refuse to be nudged along. This afternoon the sheep are elsewhere—inland, undercover or herded into pens before the storm hit.

'I was doing surgical training. Emergency medicine.'

'Why did you quit?'

The builder doesn't say anything. After a moment, Pia stops studying his profile and turns back to the road. They pass the headland and the chapel, until they are almost at the spot where she usually turns around on her run. The rain has stopped now and the sky has brightened. They pass the cottage the builder is fixing up—an old croft that had once belonged to the widow's older brother. They park in the small lot beside the hotel and the builder cuts the engine. 'How's your head feeling?'

'Okay, I think.'

'Maybe put a cold compress on it?' Then, in a voice threaded with regret, he adds, 'I'm sorry.'

Pia opens the car door and steps out. She says nothing, allows the apology to mean all the things he needs it to say.

Back in her room, Pia wets her face in the sink. On her way out of the small closet that is her ensuite, she bangs her elbow on the doorframe. Just when her body becomes accustomed to a space—an apartment, a room—and she's able to get up in the dark of night, pour herself a glass of water and make it back to bed without incident, she moves again. Over the years when other people have said the word 'home,' she felt like they were speaking a foreign language. Even at her abuela's house in the city, her room was makeshift—a mattress on low frame set up in the sewing room, a dress form on its wooden stand stationed at the foot of her bed. Pia surveys her accommodations in what would once have been the hotel's attic. It would take her ten minutes to pack. That's how little of the space she's made her own.

The hillside house that Pia's family lived in was not their own. When the family had arrived in the village by the sea, the house appeared occupied, as if the people to whom it belonged had gone out for a walk after a meal. Pia's mother paid a local woman to come in and dust and clean and wash the sheets. When Pia came across her, beating the rugs out back of the house, the woman refused to look her in the eye.

In the dining room of the hillside house there was an ornate china cabinet. One day, when she'd been living there close to a year, Pia opened a drawer, expecting to find silver. Instead she found a framed photograph. She peered at the neat little triangle of figures, thinking that they were like ghosts: a ghost in a black jacket and bow tie, another in a white dress—a woman with almond-shaped eyes and her dark hair bundled on top of her head—and another, a child-ghost standing shyly in front of her parents in a pinafore. The girl was only a few years older than Pia. All at once, Pia understood that she was sleeping in this girl's wrought-iron bed, playing with her dolls, brushing her own hair in the ghost-girl's vanity mirror.

Pia's father was from a large city to the west. He'd come to the coast to do business—hoping to start a shipping operation to support his mining interests. Where there is war there's also an economy. Pia's mother liked to remind Pia that her father had come from nothing. He'd once worked in the mines, and then in an office, and now the stack of papers on his desk, and the invoices, and his constant letter-writing signified that he was an important man. In those years Pia's father was always meeting with people, concerned with moving commodities around as fluidly as possible. He rarely had meetings inside the house, although Pia can recall once coming out of her room to find a German man in shiny black boots drinking tea at the dining room table.

Pia checks the bump on her head in her wardrobe mirror. She can't see anything between the dark parting of her hair, but the raised nub is palpable under her fingertips. Sometimes this room feels to her like that house by the sea:

she wonders who else has moved through here, what they felt gazing out the window toward the bluff, what or who they dreamt about in those nights they slept in the narrow bed. When at last she leaves for good, the room will be cleaned, the sheets washed and tucked back up to the pillow, the duvet smoothed. She imagines a strand of her hair might catch in the carpet, or that she might forget some inconsequential object: a sock, a reminder note, an old pen—ephemera released from any association with her, the person to whom it once belonged.

PIA KNOCKS ON THE WIDOW'S DOOR, shifting the dish she's cradling. A moment later, the widow appears wearing a burgundy cardigan with its buttons misaligned. 'Come in, come in,' she says, peering over Pia's shoulder as if the storm might still be raging.

Over tea the widow tells Pia that her son has come by to check on her. He'd told her that a boat had broken up, and this prompts her to tell stories about other, previous shipwrecks along the coast, every story beginning with *One time . . .* When the teapot is empty, Pia says, 'I should go,' thinking that help might be needed in the second kitchen, but the widow says, 'Have one more cup, just let me put the kettle on.' The old woman eases herself up slowly, her back hunched as she heads to her kitchen. A minute later she's back with an empty saucepan in her hand. She sets it in the middle of the kitchen table on top of the tea cozy, smiles, and says, 'There.'

One night, after the hotel bar had closed, Pia asked the barman what was wrong with the widow. He paused, the clean wine glass in his hand midway to the hanging rack, and said, 'She's just a bit lost, it happens when you get old.'

Pia was not around when her father became ill. He was a private man and kept his deteriorating health to himself. He would send her short missives that said he was busy, and asked how things were at work, did she need any money. He sent a letter every month or so and it would arrive with its foreign stamp in whatever city she was working in, and during all that time she imagined him in a sort of stasis—with a bureaucrat's busyness, orbiting concerns that had little to do with her. His last letter mentioned a course of treatment and gave a starting date, but by the time the letter was delivered he was dead.

Although the widow seems more and more confused as each week passes, she can still surprise Pia—remembering what Pia is reading, asking if she has thoughts about, say, the reign of Augustus. The last time Pia stopped by, she said, 'Every time you visit you're in the same clothes'—noticing Pia's quirks and particularities, aware of how little Pia has brought with her.

The widow's son is in his fifties. Pia spots him, gently dishevelled and glassy-eyed, in the bar some nights after her shift. He's warm and easygoing, has been on the boats since he was a kid. He once admitted to her that his parents, both well educated, had always wanted something else for him. Pia had told him about the fox she'd seen, and he was the one person who believed her. He'd shrugged and said 'this island's strange'—an observation that struck Pia as odd because she knew he'd never lived elsewhere.

The afternoon light outside the widow's kitchen has changed. The clouds are stretched into streaks, the horizon tinged with a softer blue. Pia smiles at the widow, sitting opposite her at the kitchen table, thinking that for her son it must seem as if his mother is standing on the stern of a boat that's drifting slowly away. Pia herself feels the same: how often she catches herself in a dream, as if the widow's kitchen, the window to the road, the village and the island and the mainland beyond, are evanescent, flickering.

The widow begins to say something, then stops. She taps her lips with the tips of her fingers in a gesture that's something between a blown kiss and a sign for hunger. She inspects her empty teacup, tilting her head slightly so as to rely more on her good right eye than the milky left. 'It was Livia who was really interesting, though.' The widow sighs as she says this, and smiles at Pia, and Pia recalls the references in her book on Roman history to the woman who was Augustus's wife. 'My son doesn't read at all,' the widow adds. She glances over her shoulder to the hallway that leads to the back room and all of her books. 'Is he back yet?'

'Where did he go?' Pia asks.

'To get the body bags from the town hall.'

Behind the widow, in the alcove that leads to the book room, a white cat appears. He sits, licks a paw, and pads across the carpet to settle behind a beige armchair. The widow slowly stands up again, and Pia leans forward, ready to steady her if she should start to fall.

PIA'S MOTHER DISAPPEARED TWICE. First, when Pia was twelve, at the fountain in the city plaza; and then again much later, when Pia had almost forgotten such a thing was possible. Pia was in her mid-thirties then, and working at a hotel in a large city, and happy enough, though she felt the role of entremetier was beneath her. Every night her hands smelled of raw lamb or beef, and each workday was the same as the one before. Pia's mother had taken up a position with a national news agency—working, at last, in her own language and thinking that in ten years she might retire. But her country was politically volatile, and becoming unstable.

A man phoned Pia one night, and wouldn't give his name. He said, 'Your mother is missing. Surely you're following the news?' Pia had been tuning in to the nightly reports, watching the strikes and the marches in the streets, waiting to see what would happen. A few days before, she had called home but got no answer. Her abuela was in the countryside by then, sent by Pia's mother to stay with a cousin until things settled down. Pia's father was abroad. In his last phone call he'd told Pia he was trying to get back, although flights were being cancelled, and he'd been advised it was too dangerous for him to return. Nonetheless, Pia made the trek herself. When she arrived in her mother's country, the airport was in chaos, people trying to leave, clutching their papers. And her mother was nowhere to be found.

A week later, a man appeared outside the gate of Pia's abuela's house, where Pia had taken refuge. During this week the government had come under intense pressure. It was expected to fall any day. There were troops in the streets, and the radio was broadcasting military marches. The station Pia's mother worked for was silent. One afternoon, Pia had dared to walk to the market but the darting looks she'd received up and down the street made her question if she should have ventured out. A military plane had flown across the slot of sky between the city's old colonial buildings as Pia walked quickly along. The market, when she'd arrived, was shuttered.

The man at the gate raised his arm and waved to Pia as she walked down to greet him and lifted the chain. He said, 'Your mother was my teacher'—but to Pia this sounded wrong because her mother had only ever worked as a journalist. The man was country-simple: dressed in a white shirt, pants worn through at the knees. 'You need to come with me,' he said. And for some reason she could not articulate, Pia had trusted him. She had not even thought to go back to the house for her bag or to call her father, leave a message for him.

News reports over the last few days had warned that citizens were being arrested, tortured and killed. These broadcasts had an air of panic that made them seem less than credible to Pia. But when she stood outside the city morgue with the man, these reports echoed in her mind. The man said, 'Prepare yourself.' He opened the door.

The morgue was overflowing. There were at least fifteen bodies in the entry hall—so many, some had been placed on the floors and in the small administrative offices; bodies like waste stacked in the corners of every room. Pia was taken to a door at the back of the main room and then down a set of stairs into a cold and damp basement. Bodies there were laid out on stretchers or on sheets on the floor. The sheets struck Pia as absurd: as if a body in such a state would know the difference between concrete and cotton. The stench of blood and flesh filled the room—like the smell of pigs hanging from their hooves at the butcher's. No one in the room was crying, no one was weeping over the dead. By the door a man was writing a name on a tag, attaching it to the toe of a corpse. Then he slipped the dead man's wallet into his own trouser pocket. Two dim lights had been strung from broken fixtures overhead, so that the medics, volunteers and the dead were illuminated in different degrees of darkness.

Pia could see that the bodies had been tortured: they had marks and welts and bruises. Bruises on the cheek, knives to the chest—narrow and precise stab wounds. Most of the bodies Pia glanced at were naked, or wearing only trousers or underwear, some with their hands still tied. The man closest to her had died with a spasm of agony on his face—a full jolt of physical pain.

Pia looked at the ceiling. One of the light fixtures above her had wires hanging around its empty socket. A dusty cobweb hung on the nearby ceiling fan. Three bodies separated her from her mother's. The two men closest to her had bruises around their throats. The younger man's shoulder had been pulled clear of its socket. The wrists of the woman beside her mother hung at odd angles. From her place by the door Pia could see that the white sheet covering her mother had a stain of blood the size of a dinner plate. Every cell in Pia's body told her to look away, and so she did. She stood by the door and did not go closer.

'Sí,' Pia said to the volunteer who'd brought her in, 'es ella.' Then she turned and walked away.

PIA SURVEYS THE BEACH FROM the top of the rise. Everyone is working purposefully. There are still a few hours of light left, but someone has already brought down a dozen lanterns—the ones used for the wedding—and set them up above the tide line to help people see in the coming dusk. The wood planks that are bobbing in to shore are being collected and placed in piles. A battered rowboat has been dragged up the bay and a fisherman stands over it as if he's working out a puzzle. The barman drags a net, strung with buoys, along the shore. Out in the bay a half-dozen boats motor along the coast. Earlier, the fisherman told Pia that if the bodies come in at all, it usually takes a day.

Halfway down the trail to the beach, Pia slips. She puts her hands out behind her to break her fall and ends up on her back, green-grey grass waving around her. When she rolls over to look back up the slope she spies the fox—a sideways movement toward the ridge, a flash of umber fur, then nothing. *Show yourself*, Pia thinks, staying hunched down so as not to scare her. How many generations between this fox and the ones on the fox farm decades ago? How did those who survived slip through?

When nothing happens and no fox reappears, Pia considers that she may have imagined the swift of grass, the sense of an animal's back. She remembers that it was only a few hours ago when she hit her head against the car window. She can feel a slick of cold wetness below her knee. Mud, most likely—but maybe she cut herself on a rock. *Get up*, Pia thinks—but she doesn't. 'On the fifth day of the strike,' her mother's voice echoes, '. . . It's unlikely the government will allow . . .' '. . . Overtures are being made . . .'

Once, when Pia was six or seven, her mother took her hand and marched her, irritated, toward the rise past their house on the hill. At the edge of land, above the lapping bay, she'd asked Pia: 'What do you see?' Pia's mother faced the horizon, but Pia was studying her: her yellow dress with its pearl buttons, her black hair swinging lightly over her shoulders. Pia knew then that she had agitated her mother too much, that this game—which they sometimes played when travelling—was meant to abate Pia's boredom, take care of her childish insistence on being entertained so that her mother could go back to her paper, to writing letters. Pia looked then at the glass of the sea, recalling a conversation between her parents a few weeks before, at the dining room table. Pia was supposed to be in bed but instead she sat on the stairs and listened. Her parents were talking about a local woman who believed she was being chased by a dark spirit with glinting teeth. This woman had been interrupting church services and meetings at the town hall, had shouted at four cabos who were sipping coffee at a café table. Shortly after, her body was found in the bay, and it was said she'd thrown herself into the sea from close to the spot on the bluff where Pia and her mother were now standing. Sitting on the stairs, her back to the wall, Pia had heard her mother say: 'But her bag, the shoes . . .' Some of the contents of the woman's purse, along with one shoe, had washed up, and Pia's mother said that she found it strange that anyone would jump into the sea with these unnecessary things. It would be years, no, decades, before Pia—dicing a tomato in a foreign kitchen—understood that the time she had lived through as a child in the village by the sea had been a time of terrible violence.

'What do you see?' her mother had asked. And Pia said nothing.

Now, on this island, on the slope of this hill, on her stomach with the grass swaying around her and the pieces of a boat on the tide below, she understands that her mother was asking that question of herself. That Pia was only there as a witness.

Just as Pia is bracing herself to stand up, there's a shift up the slope, between two rocks . . . slight as a change in the weather.

'Daughter of the slaughtered,' Pia whispers. On the rise, through a veil of grass, the fox lifts her head.

*O*n the land my father and his father managed, there was a large tract of forest interspersed with a half-dozen work sheds, including the one where Leonie and I went to be intimate. The woods were a utility and treated with respect, though it would be safe to surmise—from this vantage point—that my father did not know them as well as his father did. My father was, for all intents and purposes, landed gentry, and, although German, he was like a figure out of Tolstoy: walking through the workers' terrain and inquiring gently as to their methods and means with his engineer's mind. Lying in bed here on this Spanish coast, I wonder if I share my father's sense of voyeurism: a man playing at being in a world where he does not properly reside.

One of the workers on the family property was a man called Vasily. He was tall, muscular, and self-conscious of a slight stutter, though he'd meet your eye steadily in conversation. He had thick black hair and a full beard. I think, when I knew him—although he remains a grown-up in my memory—he must have been only twenty. Vasily was a foreigner, but the type to adapt quickly to the local ways and to be highly competent in his doings in order to attract the best opportunities. His job was to prune and monitor the trees to the property's best advantage. Other forests in the region had suffered from disease or poor harvests, and so my father, aware of how little a man with a family to feed would work for, paid Vasily to be a sort of caretaker to the woods. Sometimes in my wanderings I'd find him inspecting rot, or trimming branches or knifing away the mushrooms that were rooting on a fallen log. Once, however, not long after my tryst with Leonie, I saw him hurrying through a band of pines with a sack under his arm. Curious as to his purpose I followed at a distance, fancying myself a man entrusted with keeping track of my father's employees. Vasily eventually slowed down at the far side of the property, where the trees began to thin toward the river. I was almost ready to turn around, thinking he was about to leave the woods altogether, when he stopped. There, under the last stretch of canopy, a series of wooden pens had been mounted between two trees. They sat about three metres off the ground and were covered by a mossy overhang made of the same kind of shingles as the roofs of the local houses. When Vasily approached the pens, a series of high-pitched crying noises and chirpy yips ensued. I hid behind a tree and watched as he pulled handfuls of food from his sack, pressing it through the grating that covered the whole of the front. The black tips of animals' muzzles pressed through the pens' wires as he walked back and forth with the scraps. Once the sack was empty he unlooped a wineskin from under his arm and pressed some liquid into each box. The whole time his disposition was neutral, which seemed odd to me, set as it was against the whining calls and sharp barks . . . his actions were perfunctory, a task: like kicking stones off the path in front of you.

When the animals in each section of the pen had received food and water, he walked off in the direction he'd come. I had to press my back against the nearest tree and shift slightly around its bark as he walked by, so that he would not detect me. I waited, shivering with apprehension and the falling evening, counting in my head until ten minutes had passed.

There were easily thirty foxes stuffed inside eight large boxes, red foxes of the type I knew inhabited the forest. In one box was a vixen with four grey-brown kits a few weeks old. Her teats were hanging as she ate the cobs of food and scrunch of lettuce Vasily had pressed through the screen. The wood pens themselves were wet with mildew and shredded on the inside from the foxes' gnawing. I placed my fingers on the screen of one pen and the larger of the two foxes in it darted forward. I drew back just in time. The foxes' eyes were beautiful. Amber orbs with slit pupils; possessing an alertness I admired. Their noses worked the air where I stood and their bodies followed when I moved from one side to the other. I sensed they knew where I'd come from and what I'd eaten hours before; even more than that, I had a sense of being summed up: these animals see me, they're measuring the young man, the boy that I am. I guessed that Vasily was breeding them, rearing them in small enough numbers to go undetected and then selling them for pelts. A smart business if he'd trapped the first few in these very woods at no cost, mating them into an enterprise that could line his pockets with a thousand marks a year. I pictured him skinning the animals himself and selling the pelts in a village distant enough to avoid word of his venture getting back to my father. An image of Leonie and me in a shed that had been witness to such skinnings flashed into my mind, and my memory of desire in that space shamed me.

I had no tools with me, nothing useful in my pockets, and so I searched the ground until I found a palm-sized rock with a sharp end. I worked away at the thin rope that knotted the nearest pen closed, giving in to eventual frustration and using the rock to bash off the hinges instead. The foxes hid in the back of the pens while I did this and I was grateful for their cowering silence. A ruckus might have drawn Vasily back. When all the hinges were off I opened the pens, and each fox slid out like an animal darting from a nightmare into daytime. The last pen I opened contained the vixen and the pups. She did not move. Her pups stood at the edge of the box afraid to leap out. I reached in to pull the vixen by the neck and she snapped at my hand. I tallied I'd let at least twenty foxes go; all of them had disappeared now, slipped into the woods, which were humming dully. I moved my hand toward the vixen again and her back went up, her fur spiked. I took off the pullover I was wearing, wrapped it around my arm as thick as I could make it, and reached in again. She gnashed at my fingers. I gave up on her then. Breathing in deeply I turned and began to walk in the direction of the house. The walk, I knew, would take half an hour and I imagined that during this time I would debate whether or not to tell my father about Vasily. I would weigh out the consequences of the cascading events that would likely follow: his firing, resentment, possible repri-sals, and the tensions this might cause with other workers, anyone who may have been profiting from the enterprise, too. There was also the possibility my father would sup-port what Vasily was doing but demand a portion of the profit—a profit now lost because I'd acted rashly out of some romantic sentiment.

Behind me, one of the pups was whining—a sound somewhere between a hiccup and a yap. I tracked its dimin-ishing force as I walked. Five minutes on, when I could no longer hear it, I turned around. If I'm honest I would have to say that I ran back with tears in my eyes. I stood at the pens again. Every time I reached in for a pup, the vixen bit at my hand under the wrap of the pullover. But the pups were more accommodating and eventually I moved all four of them to a crop of rock the vixen might be able to dig under, far enough away that I imagined Vasily might not find them. The pups mewed in their mother's absence but then one of them, the largest, ventured a few metres away from the others, catching the whiff of something unseen. I knew that anything could happen now. The vixen might kill her pups because they carried my scent; or she might come to me, tail down, and acknowledge what had passed between us. The pups called from the rocks, and just as I returned a last time for their mother, she jumped out of the pen and darted toward them without looking back. I still have a scar on that hand. A white slash against my skin.

I RETURN TO SUZANNE AND Bernard's room around ten p.m. Suzanne is sitting in a huddle of lamplight and Bernard is awake in bed with his jacket bunched behind his head, just as it has been most nights since we left Paris. Outside, the street is empty, the moon a thin scar against a starless sky. I stand on their balcony and listen to the waves roll up onto the beach with a light *shush,* and again I'm feeling that the world—its elements—are out of touch with the disquiet of these hours and days.

Suzanne is saying that there's no chance we'll get our

documents back without them first being handed over to a garde on the French side. So we would have to take a gamble: What sort of person would this guard be, how much of a risk would they be willing to take, what else might be happening in that minute on the platform that might distract them from scrutinizing us and our papers?

Bernard has the extradition list in his hand. He smokes a cigarette and calls out names and, again, tries to place them, but we return each time to the five names we're certain of: Gaston's, Olivier's, the sculptor's, and those of the couple from the country house. Of those, the only person about whom we could offer any concrete information—an address in Marseilles, the location of his printing press, his contact in the ministry—is Olivier, our forger.

'How old is Olivier's son?' Bernard asks.

Suzanne stretches her neck and looks at the ceiling, at the unmoving fan above us. 'Seven or eight maybe; the same age as my Sebastian.'

Bernard stands and joins me on the balcony. He places his hands tightly on the railing, as if he is about to shake it loose.

'And the last time you saw Julien and Klara?' Suzanne asks.

'Where was it?' Bernard closes one eye and peers at the sky.

'The farmhouse?' I ask. 'Near Gien.'

'Ah, of course.' Bernard releases the railing. He's quiet for a minute and I sense what he's thinking—that he's remembering the same awful thing I've been trying to push out of my head since we saw Julien and Klara's names on the list. But then he laughs, surprising me, and says, 'Remember the banker? That awful man? And to think I almost forgot about him!'

The banker and his wife had appeared at the farmhouse the day after Bernard and I arrived. This was late June, when the roads out of Paris were a slow parade of cars, horses, carts and bicycles, and the occasional French soldier driving against the tide on a motorcycle or walking dejectedly toward some town he'd left when he was a different man. Everyone was barking out news and all the news was contradictory— *We are losing the war! We are winning the war!*—though the German planes overhead and the German soldiers who sometimes strafed the fields or walked alongside us until veering off to secure the next commune told the true story. In that human convoy I kept my head down and tried to be disciplined in my walking—ten minutes' walk, one minute's rest. Bernard moved through the crowds looking for someone with more certain answers than we had. Just before Ouzouer, a German plane strafed the field near where our group was walking. We ducked and hid where we could. I crouched in a ditch and felt a thin stream of water soak the knees of my trousers. A horse went down, hit by a bullet. She screamed while the man who had fallen under her called out for help. I lost track of Bernard and tried not to let that frighten me. When the planes had passed, we pushed the horse off the man and he hobbled away. None of the

French soldiers would spare the animal a bullet, and she was left to die. Eventually, the road we were walking on became impassable—filled with holes from mortars—and so Bernard and I took a byroad to get away from the bottleneck of those trying to forge south with more than just a briefcase or a simple bag.

The farmhouse appeared to be empty when Bernard and I entered it. Its main rooms had already been run through by the Germans or by looters—at least it seemed that way to us—though we also knew it was possible that someone hiding there wanted it to appear as such. We found the girl in the larder; or rather, she made herself known to us after we'd been in the kitchen rummaging around for twenty minutes and speaking French. She was fifteen or so and dressed like a peasant; wouldn't speak or answer any of our questions. Bernard surmised that she was mute—though it became apparent as our group grew that she was the only one among us with the skills the situation demanded: she knew how to kill and bleed a chicken, where to forage, how to properly knot a rope.

There was no food to be found that first day save for the chickens and hens, who had been let out of their pens earlier, but had re-entered their feeding area in goodly numbers. That night, the girl, deciding we were harmless, walked out to the barn and came back with some preserves and cold-storage items—butter and cheese—and a bottle of wine.

The banker and his wife arrived, undetected, the next night. We found them the following morning, clinging together under a white blanket just inside the garden wall. They'd given up their car the previous evening when its starter failed and had walked three kilometres through the woods until exhaustion forced them to stop. Bernard woke them with a finger to his lips and urged them inside because the white of their blanket—as dirty as it had become—was conspicuous, and planes had been flying overhead for days. There was a quick debate about whether or not they should enter—the banker wanted to go back to try to fix the car or find someone who could, though he acquiesced after his wife convinced him they needed a proper rest. 'We won't stay long,' he said, 'just until we catch our breath.' They were comical, these two—like people with impeccable manners given too few pieces of cutlery at a meal. When they came through the entry vestibule and were confronted by the coat hooks and the former owner's Turkish rug I could see the woman's face cloud with consternation—coat off, even though she was freezing? What of her muddy shoes?

From the outside, the house was every bit a farmhouse: old stone, a modest two storeys, shuttered windows, a dark green door with wicker baskets hanging on either side— their cascade of star-shaped flowers shrivelled from the sun. The house was set against an expanse of grazing fields and a large barn and covered sheds where a cow and a goat still stood. We knew the animals were a liability likely to draw attention, but even after the girl had opened the gate to the woods, they still hadn't gone anywhere.

Inside, the house was much finer than expected: the furniture, ornate and well cared for, had been covered in sheets and then uncovered and knocked over or broken to pieces. There were three bedrooms in the house—a master bedroom on the main floor with a bearskin rug and a heavy four-poster bed, a child's room upstairs, and a housekeeper's or nanny's room opposite it. Based on the size of the boy's school shoes and the well-made clothes that hung in his closet, he was probably ten or eleven. The wall of books in the large sitting room on the main floor revealed the home-owners to be people of varied interests—agriculture chiefly, but also the sciences and history. I thumbed through a number of first editions—only a half-dozen had been thrown about when the house was rummaged. One of these was a turn-of-the-century edition of Montaigne's essays which I discovered face down in the fireplace, its splayed pages reminding me of a man trying to press himself up from the ground.

My own library at that point was divided among three countries. I'd sent a number of my most important books to my parents' address where one of my cousins acted as care-taker; a second set had gone to my sister's and she, in turn, had left them with a German neighbour whom she trusted to keep them safe; a third set had stayed in my flat in Paris which the Gestapo had confiscated; and the fourth set—a grouping of ten books relevant to my work on the *Metamorphoses*—I had sent ahead to America in the hope that the overseas postal routes were still reliable. My manu-scripts—provided she had received them—were with my friend Bette in Switzerland. That this man's library was, so far, intact, gave me some form of hope.

The banker and his wife didn't leave the next morning as expected. Instead they became extremely cautious, almost paranoid. The banker got it into his head that his car had most likely been vandalized in his absence and that he was wrong to have left it. They argued constantly with Bernard about the best plan of action. The banker wanted to go back to check on the state of the automobile, taking some rope in case someone would be willing to tow it for a fee, but every time he faced the actual prospect of leaving he'd demur and say the roads weren't safe. The wife wanted to stay until the Germans passed through or the French army arrived from the south—the only two outcomes she deemed possible—but she brought such a pitch of anxiety to our deliberations that even the simplest conversations with her became unbearable. I sensed, even then, that they distrusted us. Perhaps this was because of the circles we moved in, or my accent, or perhaps they were simply more stunned than we were to be in a place of such deep uncertainty. The banker became fixated on finding a radio, as if the news out of the Vichy regime could be trusted, and so spent much of his time going back through closets and cupboards he'd rummaged through only hours before in search of the wanted technology. At least the couple seemed to understand that émigrés like me were also in a terrible situation, one that we had not brought upon ourselves. But where Bernard and the girl and I had adapted to our situation—perhaps from years of financial insecurity or from the difficulty of finding steady work—the banker and his wife were at a loss. At first, they wanted to pay for everything. The girl killed a chicken for our dinner and the banker tried to pay her as if she were the owner of the house. We gave them the largest bedroom on the main floor, with a beautiful feather-filled mattress, and they tried again to offer compensation, as if Bernard and I were entitled to that room, as if this whole debacle were temporary, like a passing cloud, and they would not need their money later.

Because we knew it was only a matter of time before the Germans came, or came back, the five of us took to staying on the main floor of the house near the kitchen, which had a large larder and two cellars. We planned to hide in the smaller cellar should anyone enter the house. The main cellar was reached by a narrow stairwell at the back of the kitchen and was the first place any thirsty soldier would look. The larder, where we first found the girl, was a decent size, but it was only protected by a wood door. The second cellar—a root cellar that was nearly empty—would fit five of us if we pressed in. Its real merit was its location—at the back of the larder, accessed by a trap door. The girl gave us the idea of affixing a number of sacks over the door with small nails, so that a soldier opening up the larder door might not know the second cellar was there at all.

Klara and Julien arrived on our fourth night in the house. Is it right to call them acquaintances? Friends? I no longer know how to describe the human beings one lives alongside, now that a sense of peril determines every action. Klara was an émigré, like me, with German parents though she was born in Warsaw. Her husband Julien was Parisian. He ran a small literary press that occasionally published artists' books. Julien had approached Bernard about his work by letter some six months before our chance meeting in the country, even though there was already tension in the cafés and streets and in casual conversations, and a sense that making any sort of professional arrangement in a time of such political unrest was futile. Like us, they had left Paris at the last minute, the two of them riding out on bicycles with their cat in a basket and bags of clothes strapped on like panniers. Their caravan, which moved slowly through the villages west of the Seine, was struck by machine guns from the air two days outside of Paris, just as they were passing alongside the discarded belongings of earlier travellers—the overturned carts, broken-down cars, abandoned mattresses and suitcases—and thought they must be nearing French troops and safety. Klara made it into the field when the gunfire started, the cat scratching her arms, and Julien hid—wedging himself as far as he could under the chassis of a Peugeot. Two weeks later, when they appeared at the door of the country house where we were hiding, Klara was still carrying that black cat . . . a creature whose lack of gratitude has stayed with me.

The evening they arrived, we were in the dining room, sitting in the near dark on cushions we'd arranged on the floor. There'd been fewer planes overhead that day, although we'd heard the occasional rifle fire—quick *rat-a-tat-tats* coming from the woods behind the property. Bernard and I were relaying our plans to the banker: we'd decided to wait another day or two and then travel by bicycle south along the minor roads. There were two bicycles out back: a man's and lady's in good condition. We'd decided to take those and try to get south of the Loire, where we believed the German advance had been stopped. The owner of the house had left his full wardrobe behind and we spent many hours deliberating what would make me and Bernard the least conspicuous—the green of the plus-fours, the brown flannel trousers, or the tweed suit? There was a three-quarter mirror on the front of the wardrobe and Bernard had tried on, first, the working coat of a landowning farmer, and then the sports jacket of the gentry, before opting finally for a knee-length overcoat appropriate for the summer weather. When we asked what the girl would do, she indicated she would remain at the house even though Bernard advised her against it, saying, 'Your hiding spot is safe, but what if the Germans come here and settle in for a while? How long can you stay down there?' It was getting dark by then. I could see the girl, her plump outline in the moonlight, but I was also tracking her breathing and what I'd come to recognize as her scent—the tang of her armpits alongside the lanolin ointment she'd been applying to a cut on her leg. What options did she have? She was young, alone, and couldn't—or wouldn't—speak. Even when she'd knocked her knee on an end table one night she hadn't made a sound.

The banker's wife was on lookout that evening, sitting on an embroidered footstool and peering out the base of the window at the front of the house. Suddenly there were two quick taps on the front door. We all looked at her, but she shook her head to say she'd seen nothing. I stood up, moved across the room to the door, but couldn't bring myself to open it. The knob rattled as whoever was outside tried to enter, but the door was locked. I heard muffled voices and I think it was this—the sense that people were talking, speaking to each other, not yelling or commanding—that led me to open the door despite Bernard whispering *non* behind me. *Whatever comes, comes,* I thought—which I now realize is horrible because it wasn't only my life at stake.

'Oh, thank God,' Klara said, almost falling over the doorstep, her coat winging open as she staggered forward, its satin lining shining in the moonlight. Julien stepped in after her and closed the door, and Klara slid down the length of it and started sobbing. I could see in the grey light that her hair had leaves in it and that there was a gash on her forehead. Something poured forth from her arms, and I stepped back thinking she was bleeding—but it was only the cat, who began to rub his back along my trouser legs.

Julien was out of breath but still standing. 'We were watching you,' he said, 'from the woods. You have to be more careful when you go out for the chickens.'

What Klara brought with her, for those few days we were together, was a language only she and I could speak, and a shared sense of anguish at our internal division—that we were 'them' but not 'them,' that we were labelled boches even though a part of us had felt at home in France, felt some form of identity that transcended borders and the madness of the times. We discovered one night, halfway through a bottle of Sancerre—compliments of our absent host's cellar—that we both dreamt in multiple languages. Klara dreamt in French unless she dreamt of her mother, and then the dreams were in German. I said that I dreamt in three languages—though thinking about it later in the boy's bed, I realized that in some ways my dreams were more like thematic bursts than scenes acted out in words. We spoke about our parents then, and when she described her mother she stood up from the chair in the sitting room and marched and huffed around, doing her best impression of a strict matron with a thick neck and heavy chin complaining about the quality of the bockwurst in the market. I laughed for the first time in weeks.

The banker and his wife left the next morning. The house had become too crowded and the banker's concern for his car had risen to the point where leaving it on the side of the road any longer was, to his mind, insane. In a world of diminishing assets everyone became attached to the one thing they felt could sustain them: a car, an ungrateful cat, books.

I remember watching the girl the night Klara marched around speaking German—her face was a white saucer in a dark room, full of distrust. Klara's accent, my accent, our words too strange. Even in the mornings, when I would sit in the kitchen on cushions to read in the sunlight coming through the high windows, the girl seemed wary of me . . . though it might also have been a wariness of books, of the mysterious worlds I was seeing in there. I had borrowed the owner's copy of Ovid's works, a lovely edition with Middle English on the left side of the page and French on the right. It was a translation I hadn't seen before and I was interested to discover how some of my favourite stories had been interpreted. I tried to explain what I was reading and asked the girl if I could read to her. She nodded indifferently, so I read a few pages. I remember her mouth flicking up into a smile when I read about Echo, the cursed nymph who could only repeat the last parts of other people's phrases: 'Come here, and let us meet!' Narcissus called. 'Let us meet!' Echo answered. I wasn't used to reading aloud to others, not since those last years with my brother, but the more I dramatized things the more she responded, and in those hours I felt my childhood come back to me.

We never did find out if the girl could speak or if she simply chose not to. Bernard said that once, watching her sleep in the afternoon on the floor of the kitchen, he was sure he heard her whimper. She liked Bernard the best. He had found some games—chess and backgammon—in the boy's room upstairs and he played these with her in the evenings, sitting on blankets near the larder door and our precious second cellar. One night after the banker and his wife had left and something approximating calm had come back to the farmhouse we, all five of us, played a record on the lowest possible volume and waltzed around.

I can still see the girl's open expression as she swayed in Bernard's arms, so sweetly self-conscious but happy. The day we were preparing to leave she was shot in the yard trying to collect one of the chickens. A long-distance shot from the road. I refused to let anyone out to drag her back in, but in my defence, she wasn't moving. No, that's a lie. That's what I said to Klara and Julien and Bernard, and to myself, when we rushed into the cellar to hide. *She's not moving.* Even as her arm swept across the dirt like someone waving goodbye.

BERNARD HAS FALLEN ASLEEP. I ask Suzanne if we should wake him, and she gives me a look that says we two will decide what happens next.

Suzanne is, of the three of us, the one I trust to make decisions. For months she's been helping people navigate their way to the border from Marseilles: helping those who couldn't get the right papers, who had no visas, who'd heard from someone who'd heard from someone else that she had good connections in the south of France and knew a route over the mountain. But she was also in danger because of this. Her contact at the tabac in Banyuls told her that word had come from Suzanne's husband Artun in Paris that a German man in plain clothes had come to their apartment to inquire as to her whereabouts. As well, a mutual friend in Vichy had said that her name had appeared on a list of 'people of interest' to the regime. Before this, her papers had meant that she was free to travel. 'Artun now wants you to go to America,' the contact had said, sliding a transit visa across the table in the back room of the tabac. 'If you don't go to America now,' he'd said, 'well, even you aren't safe.' And then he'd looked at Bernard and me, and shrugged. Suzanne told me on the walk up the col that she'd debated: Should she go with us? Wait a day, or more? Were there others she could help? But Bernard was ill and she hadn't left his side since Artun had arranged for us to meet with her in Marseilles, so she'd decided to stay with us as least as far as Lisbon.

The list of names Herr Gabler gave us is on Suzanne's lap. I sense she's trying to memorize as many as she can in case she finds herself in a position where she can warn or get word to the people on it. This is where we differ. Suzanne still thinks she can make a difference; I'm not so sure.

Bernard stirs and I realize it's possible he's not been sleeping at all. He blinks up at the ceiling. 'Is there anything we can give them?' he asks. 'A lie even, that will make it look as if we're cooperating?'

I relay what Alejandro had said to me outside the restaurant—that a man who had offered information had been allowed to proceed through Spain.

'Do you believe him?' Suzanne looks dubious.

I remember Alejandro's face as he fed me the soup, how I did not hesitate to take the food. 'Yes.'

'So, what can we safely offer?' Suzanne asks.

We debate what's possible: knowledge of Gaston's academic work? Details of my last contact with him when I was released from the camp in Nevers? An old address of Olivier's in Marseilles . . . or maybe a false address? But then, what of the people who may actually live at that address? We agree that anything we say opens the door to a possibility of harm—even if the reverberations of a simple lie exceed our current imaginations. And more than that, more selfishly, any admission may accidentally implicate ourselves.

'Exactly,' Suzanne says, 'any knowledge of Olivier, true or false, means that we know a forger—which is admitting that some of our documents may not be real.' She is pacing now, and this starts to annoy me.

'So,' Bernard says, 'in the morning you go to Porras or Estévez or whomever and say we cannot help. It's done.'

The look on Suzanne's face says no. I turn to Bernard and see he has now reached the place I reached back at the farmhouse: *Whatever comes, comes.* I'm sorry to see him in this place, when I think he still has the ability to live.

Just as we are discussing our plan of action, we hear a noise from the room next door. It's as if a desk or table has been knocked against the wall nearest us—and so we stop speaking. This is the room where light was coming out from under the doorframe. We turn to the wall and listen, hear three quick taps. After a minute Suzanne says, 'I'll go.'

'Go where?' I ask.

And Suzanne replies, 'I'm going to knock on that person's door and ask them if everything's okay. Then at least we'll know who's in there.'

When Bernard came for me in Paris, German soldiers were closing in on the city. It was early June, maybe the ninth or tenth. I remember walking down from my apartment on Dombasle to get my customary coffee and croissant at the patisserie on the corner only to find the locals smiling stiffly and Vivienne, the girl behind the counter—who worked part-time because she was studying chemistry at the university—with two blooms of colour on her cheeks. When I asked if everything was all right she whispered, 'Everyone's saying that the Germans are at the city's door.'

I arrived home from the library that evening to find Bernard standing by my bookshelf perusing a copy of Fichte's *Doctrine of Scientific Knowledge*.

'Who let you in?' I asked.

'I let myself in,' he said, 'when Claudette came out.'

Claudette was another tenant in the house, a student from Lyon. 'How was she?'

'Nervous.'

I glanced at my cramped kitchen and thought about offering him tea, but then remembered I'd run out the week before.

'Maurice has been arrested,' Bernard said. 'I've been told they're going to round up the whole group. Not me, but all of you from the philosophical society.' He rubbed his eyes with his fists. 'It's serious this time. Not like a volunteer camp where a good letter can get you out.' He put his hand on the fireplace mantel and I almost laughed because he looked like a parody of the dishevelled young Romantic—the exact sort of portrait he would despise. I could tell my expression exasperated him because his eyes narrowed. 'Listen: they're arresting people,' he said briskly. 'If you're going to go, if *we're* going to go, we need to go now.'

I've never been sure why Bernard came for me that day—why me, in particular . . . or why he helped me out of the camp months before that. And I have had hours upon hours to think, between the camps and the farm-house and now, about what binds us. His story will, no doubt, be different than mine. Why he loves me—if we are to call it love—will likely hinge on some encounter or set of words I do not recall. For me, I think of that moment I observed him outside the church with his head bent back and the gargoyles pawing the air above him. Perhaps, for him, it is the fact that I sought him out when the others had gone, staggering on to their next party, or to whatever art event or next instance of satisfaction awaited them. Did I love him then, that day he came to warn me in my apart-ment in Paris? No. I loved what I have always loved—the question *why*. When he stood in the daubed light of the church, his face studying its fascia, he was like the answer to a question. In that moment, I was also taking him inside me. That is what looking does: his rapt face, his desires and his loneliness came through him into my consciousness— and I saw a loneliness I understood too well.

Suzanne returns to the room and a man walks in behind her. He's tall, with tightly curled hair, a squat nose, features that seem familiar. Before anyone speaks I can picture him in the tabac by the station in Banyuls—the man in the back room who moved past us as Suzanne's contact slid the vineyard workers' hats under the table.

'This is Philippe,' Suzanne says. 'He's Jean-Claude's brother.'

Bernard sits up in bed and he and I nod in greeting.

'Jean asked me to come after Suzanne phoned him yesterday,' says Philippe. 'We travel through this hotel frequently on business, so my presence won't raise an alarm. Has the guard come by yet? He was due ten minutes ago if he keeps to the hour.'

Bernard shakes his head. 'We haven't seen him since we came back.'

Seemingly conscious that he is towering over us, Philippe sits in the chair nearest the foot of the bed. 'I've brought money for a bribe. Artun will pay it back to us after all this is over.' He hands Suzanne a brown paper bag. 'Estévez is the one to give it to. We've heard he's let people go, waved off papers, looked the other way. As commissioner he's lining his pockets with this war. The reason he keeps coming to the coast is because he's getting rich here.'

Suzanne opens the end of the bag and thumbs through the money. I listen for any sound in the hall but the hotel is quiet.

'Once he has the money, ask Estévez to send you back on the train. He should be able to arrange for a certain French guard to take you from the train in Banyuls. The guard will act as if he's extraditing you but he'll let you go outside the station. You'll have your papers but will be on foot from there.'

I could see Bernard's expression in the dim light—a flare of hope. I wondered: Is this what it's like to be a painter? Each new stroke of the brush opening up a new possibility? I remembered a work Bernard made after we stayed two days at a chateau north of the Loire. A gift to the woman who owned the house and who let us stay in her barn even as the German soldiers came and went, working their way through her food stores and wine cellar and, I suspected, her. Her son, nowhere to be seen, had a selection of watercolour paints. One night after the Germans had gone back to their base, she offered the paints to Bernard and as thanks he made a conjecture of her on a thick sheet of paper—an image of her standing in her floral blouse by the main stairs. The whole scene was a work of the imagination, but when it was done I had to stop myself from weeping—he'd caught her form and quiet bravery exactly: her long neck and loose hair; eyes like rippling pools.

After Philippe goes back to his room and Suzanne has hidden the money, we devise a plan for the morning. Alejandro—no doubt sleeping lightly in the lobby through our quiet comings and goings—is to take us to the police station at ten. Suzanne will ask for Estévez, and once she is alone with him she'll offer him the bribe and, if necessary, some innocuous information about Gaston: an address he briefly held in Paris, a false sighting on the streets of Marseilles.

I GO TO MY ROOM, TO BED. What do I dream in these hours? Am I even asleep? Or do I lie awake? I've come to the point where both forms of consciousness bleed into each other. I'm like someone running a fever all of the time. I'm thinking now, under my thin blanket, of love. It's a humiliation, to always be thinking of food or love. One reaches a stage, a kind of near-death consciousness, where sentiment sweeps in. Or if not that, then the desire for order and meaning and purpose, the need to ask what it's all been for. This leaves me bitter. I think now, in my discomfort, of those sated by love: the swimmers out in the bay yesterday moving toward and away from each other, and the father and son at the café—and even you, Pia, and your mother, who took your hand on the passeig two days ago. I think of wilful human entanglement and it makes a part of me rage and a part of me die. Have I known such love? I have. I've had my own parents, my sister—even as she grew remote. I've had Salomé and a few others, and a community of like-minded thinkers who would have worried about my absence on a Sunday when usually we met over coffee. I ask myself here and now, What is the thrust of love? And in my bed, in this derelict light, I think that its meaning is to see another naked, to see another without all their faces tried on and taken off. The peasant girl who could not give us her name exemplified this. And so, Pia, do you. Ask me why I don't get up and take the tablets now, and I would tell you that it's not because I am hoping that Estévez will help—I don't believe he will. I've seen his sort before: selfish and cruel. Rather, I'm still working out an equation. These are the three pieces: love, Narcissus, and you, Pia. Love, Narcissus, and you.

I wake in the night, as I always do, and struggle in those first few minutes of wakefulness to locate myself exactly. I know that I am here, in a bed in Portbou—but even with that knowledge I feel less obdurate, less present than the dresser or the rickety chair outlined in the dark. I have had periods of conflict, of indecision. But, until now, I have always felt grounded, like a man who has thrown down stakes, who has invested in his position, his momentum. Those days are gone. Now my energy is elsewhere. How strange, Pia, that you should be more real to me than the curtains framing the balcony past my feet, or the stem of moonlight pressing through their folds.

It occurs to me now that under different circumstances, the Middle English version of the Narcissus story—the one that I read in the farmhouse in Gien—would have informed my work. How, even in those dire circumstances, I was excited to discover new things in that translation . . . for example, how the landscape that Narcissus moves through is more powerful than he. When Narcissus loses sight of his hunting companions and begins to look for them, danger is everywhere: the mountains are steep and grey, the pine forest thick, the cave mouths foreboding. Even Echo's querying voice comes as a shock as he stands nervously in the glade.

Still, the farmhouse version had all the markers of Ovid's influence: Narcissus is between states—we're told he is neither a man nor a boy, that he is a good hunter but that the deer he drives into his nets are easy prey. But it differs from the original in two key ways: First, in its description of the woods. In Ovid's telling, the spring is 'a clear pool' and the clearing 'undisturbed by bird or beast,' but in the later, more realistic version, the glassy water is alive with pond fish and the woods are thick with chatter. A stag stares in wonderment, his flank wet from a recent rain. The Middle English writer brings us closer to the event through a form of sympathy: clouds gather, the sky begins to weep. It is not only Narcissus's tears that disturb his reflection in the pool, but the elements themselves. His dissolution belongs to the physical world: the pond fish flicker below him, the reeds sway, a bee lifts off the lip of an iris, a goshawk swoops over the glade with a vole in its talon, a fox steps out between pines.

The second difference between the two versions has to do with Narcissus himself. In Ovid's telling, Narcissus believes that he and his reflection are two separate people: '. . . whenever *I* lean forward to kiss the clear water *he* lifts up *his* face to mine and strives to reach *me*.' But in the translation I found in the farmhouse, Narcissus peers into the pond—sees the veil of water that keeps him from himself—and acknowledges his duality: '*I*, who am the seeker, and *I* who am the sought.' It struck me, as I read these words, that he was experiencing the deepest form of rupture: a self that is both fragmented and whole.

The sound outside my window in Portbou is of the sea, its gentle meeting with the shore. There's none of the nighttime street noise typical of the cities I've lived in, and common before the war, when people lived expansively. I shift my legs in the bed and the left leg begrudges the movement. I know my heart isn't what it ought to be, but the left leg's reticence these past months is a mystery. To will the body and have it refuse you is a strange thing because it makes you, like our friend Narcissus, see yourself doubly: as both self and obstinate other.

There have been times these past months when I've wondered how close I am to death—even without my tablets. How many years would Meira say I have left if she saw me now? I remember one afternoon back at the camp des travailleurs volontaires in Nevers, I woke from a nap in the courtyard to discover a young man trying to yank my boots off. I felt a tug on one foot and then my eyes flew open— first to grey sky and a crown of tree leaves, and then to the tousled top of a man's head. He tugged again, this time harder. When I kicked him he startled and jumped back, raising his hands in the air. He explained that he had looked closely and thought I was dead. He said his name was Joseph and he was there with his brother Aaron. He stepped back and a young man in a thin sweater appeared. They were in their twenties—twins, I think, for both had thick brown hair, wide-set eyes and broad shoulders. What could I say then? 'I'm not dead'? I said nothing. I was struck by this double vision, but also struck by the idea that there was work to be done, that because I was still alive it might fall to me at some point to take the boots off of some other man, to try to decide if he were dead or merely sleeping. In many ways I'm glad I'm not that man now—the man who must act. I have so little left it's almost not worth measuring.

Now it is dawn, and I'm out on the balcony trying to assess what part of the past six hours has been sleep, and what part has been thinking. I keep picturing the jug in Suzanne and Bernard's room. How close I was to asking them if I might borrow it to wash up. It was similar to the jug I dropped in the lobby: handmade, a fine shade of blue. Outside the gulls are awake, such clamouring. They swoop and brake over the shore, then lilt out toward the sea. I light a cigarette, my second last, as if I'm a man on holiday. I have no notion what day it is, though I suspect it's Sunday. The church bell has yet to chime but the streets are quiet and without any hint of industry. I reach down and scratch at my ankle. The bite marks that were pinpricks two days ago are getting larger. Last night I caught myself scratching at my calf a number of times. The insistence with which I kept at it reminded me of a dog repeatedly bringing his hind foot up to his ear—the sort of automation that made medieval philosophers think animals lacked souls. Now my two welts are almost the size of quail's eggs. I thought at first they might be bedbug bites but it's more likely they're spider bites from up on the col, from the hour we spent resting by the rocks. It doesn't matter, except that I've come to like this hotel bed, and bedbugs would be a disappointment. It's been weeks since I've had the pleasure of the same bed for more than one night—and while this mattress feels as though it's filled with wood boards and old clothes, it's still better than the floor.

At seven, I hear the sound of a tray dropped outside the door. Bread and oil. This is the diet of the famine. Everywhere, women make bread, and Europe's stock of olive oil seems to be endless. I'm not hungry, though I think of food constantly. My daydreaming is full of tension: between food that is elaborate to think about—the coq au vin from Martine's, Salomé's gougère, the cured meats at the market—and what food is actually possible. The olives the day before yesterday were a treat. The salad at the Paradou disappointed even as it sated me, and the meal at El Dorado tasted like cardboard because the charade made one feel sick.

The passeig below me is quiet. I make a little catalogue of the hour: no one swims, the bay laps, a man in farmer's clothes walks down the street toward the hills. A set of shutters is pushed open, conversation burbles up from an unseen courtyard; a young man rides past on a bicycle. After several minutes, people start to appear, dressed for church even though the church when we passed by it was partly destroyed, almost all of the statues on its fascia missing heads or hands or feet. We've been told that in this part of the country the bells are rung when someone in the village dies, regardless of the hour, and in this way everyone knows a death has occurred. I imagine the bellman must be tired.

I admire how the birds of Portbou do not flock. How they stand their corners. No one is throwing bread to them, no one cares if they survive. Each has a particular degree of tenacity. There is one gull in particular I have been watching— he flies back and forth from the arm of the bench facing the sea up to the roof above me. He's dirty grey and sharp beaked, and he seems to be saying to all the others, *This man belongs to me.*

When I see you, Pia, you are wandering down the passeig ahead of your parents. Your mother is wearing a blue print skirt and white blouse, and your father is dressed in a casual suit. You have a pink bow in your hair, which doesn't suit you. Your parents are talking as they stroll along, your father listening to your mother intently. I see again that she has the sort of expressive face an artist would admire.

As you near the beach, you begin to run. I knew you'd be good at this, like my sister. When I was a child she could run from our house to the distant neighbour's and not get tired— unlike me. So, here you are, your legs pumping, arms swinging loosely at your sides. First, you head down the passeig itself, picking up speed, and then you veer onto the pebbly beach. Before your mother notices, you've already sprinted halfway toward the lip of water. When she calls you, you look back over your shoulder, but you don't stop running until the toes of your shiny black shoes reach the sea. I remember what it's like to watch someone run like that—thrusting themselves forward—full of the wonder of what the body can do.

You return to your mother when she calls for you, and she bends down and inspects your shoes. Then she lifts you, a squirming five-year-old . . . taking in, as mothers do, the measure of you in this moment, the heft of you in her arms.

In Ovid's poem, the version of himself that Narcissus falls in love with is both insubstantial—'a mere shadow'—and a real entity with all the qualities of a self. Narcissus sees himself, his true self, outside of his own body. Those of us who have come through these last few months also know what it is to fracture. One day you live in the familiar world and the next you are carrying your meagre allotment of things and the landscape is changing and your legs are heavy as stone, and you are squatting to shit on the side of the road next to a mattress and a jumble of clothes someone tipped off their cart weeks ago. And then you are walking up to a farmhouse outside a village where all the men have fled and the women are wide-eyed and fearful. And in this spate of days and weeks, the old life becomes the dream. Neither is more real than the other, except that one is the above-water version, and the other has been pulled under—one is the face of a man who no longer recognizes himself; the other is the face of a man submerged.

Bernard and I left the country house near Gien a few hours after the girl was shot. When no one came for the chickens or for us, we snuck out a secondary door on the far side of the house nearest the shed and the barn. We thought that if we could get the bikes from the shed, we could walk them to the woods after dusk and then ride out onto the road. The house no longer felt safe. I went first, moving across the yard, avoiding the sight of the girl, clasping my briefcase in my arms. I told Bernard to wait. In the shed, I took the woman's bike and wheeled it to the barn. This was the span of space where I expected a bullet would kill me. The stench in the barn was shocking. There were six horse stalls along the wall and no horses visible. They had probably been shot, or died of thirst or hunger if no one had time to free them. A swarm of flies buzzed violently. I turned and saw Bernard standing behind me with the man's bike. He retched at the smell and a semblance of the eggs he'd had for lunch slopped onto his knees. I covered my nose with the palm of my hand. It must have been around five or six p.m.—ludicrous shafts of afternoon sunlight came in through the barn's doors, some of the flies buzzing up and down in its vents. I saw the brown shoes first, then his trousers and grey sweater stretched at the neck; and her swollen legs, her skirt resting above her knees, her blue blouse torn. There were bullet holes in their foreheads: her hair matted, his beard thick with blood. He was staring straight out the stall door, and our eyes almost met as they had when I'd stared through the glass at his family photograph. The dark-haired boy was huddled in the corner, in a knit vest and navy trousers, his face against the stall wall. The blood on his back was black and tarry. What had this family done? Refused the Germans entry? Refused to open their house up? Some small act of protest? Or maybe they'd tried to run.

How long would I have stayed there, looking, if Bernard had not yanked my arm, pulled me back into the world we were moving through? I had slept in this boy's bed, pressed my face into his pillow. I had worn this man's coat, taken his unoffered hospitality. I had run my finger over the spines of his books, eaten the preserves this woman had made. I had waltzed and laughed in their living room. I had a thought, then—a certainty: that what I had seen would create inside me another person . . . that the man who would soon exit the barn and walk toward the woods would not be the same man who'd entered it.

WHEN I ENTER SUZANNE AND Bernard's room, Bernard is standing by their basin washing his hands, an empty breakfast plate beside him. Suzanne tells me she wants to follow Philippe's advice and bribe Estévez, even though we agree that Estévez has given no indication that he's susceptible. It's a move in a game of chess—a game where we always seem to be outwitted. Bernard says we should go along with Philippe's suggestion—'What do we have to lose?'—and so he casts his lot in with Suzanne and the money being lent to us. Suzanne is wearing her brown dress. She has softened her hair and applied lipstick. She could be any woman on the streets of Paris before the war, except for the fact that she's carrying a belt of money around her waist.

'I think it's best if I meet Estévez alone.' She smiles as she says this, but her expression is fragile and only serves to make her appear more vulnerable.

'Don't—' Bernard says, but can't voice the rest of it. I know he is remembering how Estévez looked at her, like a pig at a trough.

'The money is enough,' Suzanne assures us, and she smiles again and pulls on a pair of leather gloves I'd forgotten she had. Gloves that transport me to more civilized times, to my mother leaving for dinners, to my aunt at the end of my twelfth birthday dinner buttoning up each loop along her wrist before stepping outside, to Salomé one night in winter shuddering in a cab because her hands were so cold and allowing me to slide my woollen gloves over her pale fingers.

And so we let Suzanne do it. It's daytime, after all: a day with the absurdity of sky and beach and families walking around on a Sunday, and the church opening its doors.

From the balcony, Bernard and I watch Suzanne walk down the passeig. We see Alejandro's cap, how he waves at her and the cabo who has come for her. The bay is sparkling, though the sea beyond the headlands is choppy, dark blue. Bernard disappears into the closet and comes back with a bottle of Spanish brandy. The look of surprise on my face clearly delights him. 'It's helping with my congestion,' he says.

'Alejandro?' I ask.

'The widow,' he replies. 'Though she's a better haggler than you'd think.'

I take two chairs and move them toward the balcony while Bernard plucks the cork out of the bottle and pours two measures of brandy into the water glasses on his night-stand. When he sits down he says, 'Try not to think about it. Suzanne's smart. And she's done better than most.'

I try to think of 'the most' to whom he's referring. The woman in the chateau south of the Loire? The one who fed the Germans lunch when they came knocking, and whom he'd painted using her son's watercolours?

'What does a man like Estévez want?' Bernard asks. He crosses his ankles and my gaze falls onto his scuffed shoes. 'Money or power?'

I laugh half-heartedly. 'You don't think that these two things are the same?'

We talk about Olivier. The fact that visas from Marseilles were cancelled could mean the Germans know that some-one is forging visas there, forging every document—for Olivier had managed, through a contact in the Vichy gov-ernment, to get copies of almost every new form the Germans invented. In his studio there were safe-conduct passes, transit visas, exit visas—all of them used as sparingly as possible and only in the direst situations. He even had a prescription pad, so that medicine could be procured from any pharmacy still operating; he did everything, it seemed, but passports.

'A man like Estévez wants Olivier,' I say. Estévez is, after all, the Commissioner of Information—a man stuffed between a desk and chair in Madrid, and a man who must occasionally rouse himself to come up to the border areas in a show of solidarity with his German guests. What does Estévez care about émigrés or refugees coming out of France if they keep going all the way to the ports of Lisbon? He has his own problems here, he is still sweeping up his own messes. He strikes me as a man who likes money and food and women, who likes the way other men look at the sleek lines of his automobile when it pulls up to a restaurant, who enjoys how his coat hangs off his shoulders as the driver opens his door.

'But does he want Olivier more than the money Suzanne's offering him?' Bernard asks.

This is a question neither of us can answer.

While we wait for Suzanne, we talk about Paris. Now that Bernard thinks he is about to move forward—or at least go back to France in order to try this manoeuvre again—he's nostalgic: he reminisces about the dancer he liked to watch at Le Gerny, the weeks he spent painting at the slaughter-houses at La Villette. He's thinking, it seems, mostly of subjects for his work. This annoys me.

'What would you miss most?' I ask.

He raises his chin.

'On this earth, I mean.' I gesture to the swath of sea and sky before us.

He takes a swig of brandy. 'Kissing, I think.' Then he laughs. 'Do you remember your first? How it felt? My first was—' He stops and leans forward, remembering it. 'Do you know this painting called *L'Apparition*? It was going around Paris three or four years ago? In it there's a man, a painter, dressed in rich colours, his little foot on a precious stool as he paints . . . and over his shoulder this angel has appeared, all muscle and feather on a cloud. And everyone who sees this painting—even your Salomé, as I recall—thinks it's about art and holy visions . . . but I saw the painting and I thought, no, that artist is looking at the angel's massive cock. Well, my first kiss was like that, like some sort of bodily revelation.'

Bernard stands up and takes a cigarette from the bedside table. I can't see how many he has left. 'And you, professor? What would you miss most?'

It's strange, this question, because I feel like I should have already tread these thoughts—but I haven't. I have sensed my own death so palpably, felt it walk with me since yesterday, or the day before, perhaps even since the farmhouse near Gien, yet now I feel that all the answers I could construct, all the memories that grounded me, are insubstantial—like bridges one can no longer cross. And so, to cover my embarrassment, I describe a day trip: walking up to a medieval hilltop town from an Italian lake. The surprise of the exertion. In my telling, I'm a young man—in my thirties—arriving at the edge of the town just as dusk is settling. I joke about the want of nothing more than a good bed. But under my narration, I'm thinking of what it means to be loved. To love. Under my description of the blanket of stars and the hotel owner of La Terrazza naming a price that gave me no pause on account of my flagging legs, I am thinking that no experience in this world matches being seen by someone who loves you, and that this, these exquisite moments, are what I'll miss. Just as I feel this fully, I stop talking, and Bernard reaches out and grabs my hand.

I stand up, light-headed. I see that Bernard has smoked his last cigarette—a gesture that seems both defiant and optimistic. He does look stronger today. For the first time I notice a hint of his curls coming back, and this makes me happy. Under his breath he is humming a song I don't recognize. Despite everything, he looks like a man at ease. When I think back on all my years in Paris, all the weekly gatherings at the café, Bernard does not figure as largely in my memory as he should. He was on the outside of the circle. He was the one who would appear out of nowhere, bringing an extravagance: the invitation to Salomé's in Vienna, a ticket for a play, a day at the races where, flush from some commission, he paid for all of his friends' bets. I tried to talk to him once, on the road out of Paris, about Narcissus. This was back when I was fooling myself into thinking Narcissus was a small part of my work on the *Metamorphoses* and not, somehow, the central thing. Bernard listened politely, which was typical of his disposition, though I don't think he understood me. Perhaps it's because he's a painter. In his work, transformation is a given: the one who sits for their portrait becomes the one who looks out through the paint. But I'm starting to think that this notion of transformation is too simple. Too simple because transformation requires a then and a now; a linear understanding. Some might say we are moving forward but I would say we have regressed—we have gone back to the place we have been before, we are standing again at the foot of our own barbarity, our wreckage. Where Bernard and Suzanne see a chain of events, see possibility, I see the same repeating catastrophe: the violence behind us, the violence yet to come. I would like to do something about this, but I find myself helpless. I am caught up in the swell of an idea: that I do not want to live to see the things I think others will see.

Still, I believe that small gestures matter. This is why I go back again and again to my pen and paper; to you, Pia. And it is why I have tried to look with such attention at the world—yes, to find something, or someone, to save me; but also to find someone, or something, I can save.

I walk over to the basin by the wall and take Suzanne and Bernard's jug in my hands. I ask Bernard if I can borrow it to wash up. He says, 'Of course.'

In the washroom closet down the hall I splash my face and rinse the jug and fill it with water from the tap. I squint in the little square mirror hanging from a hook above the sink and I see the heavy circles under my eyes, the folds of my flesh, the pallor of a man who is ill. I picture Suzanne with her skirt up around her hips and Estévez behind her thrusting and then I shake the image from my head, close the door and go back to my room.

PIA, THERE'S ONE MORE version of the Narcissus fable I've been turning over in my mind. It was translated from Greek into French by an abbess in the twelfth century. It's called the Mytilene manuscript, and it tells of Narcissus's mother, Liriope, a nymph who was taken forcefully by the river god Cephisus. A god who 'wrapped her in his powerful stream, imprisoned her in his currents and ravished her forcefully.' This is rape. And it means that Narcissus was a child born of violence.

Echo is considered more wholly in this version, too. We are reminded she once had a body and a voice and that she could speak as she liked about the world. The Mytilene manuscript suggests that *not* being able to state how you feel or what you see is a kind of torture.

There is one more distinction in this version. The Mytilene manuscript, rather than show Narcissus wither, has him take his own life.

κλαἰύςατο δ' ἀγλαΐην
] . . . δῶκε δὲ γαίηι
] . . . φέρειν

Within a spring; he wept for his beauty.
Then the boy shed his blood and gave it to the earth
. . . to bear.

The tablets have no taste, almost no residue, which makes me worry they won't do the work I want them to do. I ask myself to name this work, and the word that comes to mind is *erasure*. All morning I've flirted with the idea that I'm not human anymore—that if I try to report what I've seen, the path that lies ahead, I'd choke on the words as my mouth tried to form them. I think of the blind seer Tiresias prophesying of Narcissus, *He will live a long life as long as he doesn't come to know himself.* I take off my shoes and I feel my vacancy. I loosen the top button on my shirt and I feel my vacancy. I picture my cousin Leonie, her white breasts and pert nipples, the mouse I bashed with a log, my brother with his mouth slung open after being spoon-fed, Salomé straddling me on her blue sofa, the dead girl amongst the chickens; I picture the father, mother and the little boy in the stall out back of their house, and I feel my vacancy. It's like being impossibly empty and impossibly full at the same time.

My briefcase and my money are in the closet with a note for Bernard. I will not apologize. Perhaps he'll take the work that I've been doing on Ovid and make something of it, place it in the right hands. But if my ideas are lost, so be it.

If anything, I regret not having a new thought about bridges and forms—which my thesis adviser demanded of me. I tried. For a while I thought I had it—the idea of signifying things, material stories, how the past abides in traces—how the wear on the stone steps of one bridge gathers the soles of a century. But when I left Paris these thoughts receded, and other concerns came to the fore, and it felt quaint to imagine that in some other life of mine I'd stood in wonderment before a piece of architecture. But how else do we remember? Even our stories are stuffed with *things*.

What I now think I have missed is the idea of time welling around and through those things we use to order the world—the bridge that brings order to space, that brings a geometry of relief to two verges of land while also holding time, making time—even the gap between you and me, Pia—perceptible.

I was told to expect hallucinations. And slowly, even with my eyes closed, they come. The square of light from the balcony becomes a sky through which a bird flies. And the shadow by the closet becomes the doctor who gave me the pills, though he refuses to come toward me. The bed is a boat lightly bounding on a sea. I hear a knock on the door and even though I know it's a fleeting figment I say, to whoever is out there, 'Come in.'

And then, in the corner of the room: a girl in a tree, laughing! Then a wave of warmth that is Salomé, and then another, more innocent one, that is my mother. I reach out to touch her sad face. Then suddenly I am in Saint-Germain at the café and having great ideas and these ideas are like sparks in my brain and someone has ordered a wine I haven't tried—a Baron Philippe de Rothschild!—and I'm really tasting it: the degree of sun on the grapevines, how it was garrotted, the soil of the valley it came from, the trace of spice and pepper on its dark fruit like a ghostly outline. And here is Gaston looking at my face as if I take everything too seriously . . . and again I see him walk across the street to pick up a napkin that the wind has sent to the nearby hedge, how as he comes back to us he's waving that white flag over-head. And I see you, Pia, with your pert, smart face. You as a girl and you as a woman. And even though I'm alone I feel strangely held by you, through the far side of the mirror, as if you're saying *I will see you to the last.*

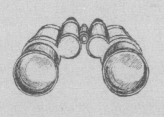

*P*ia's ears are ringing. The builder rolls over beside her in the early morning light, drops his right arm over her ribcage and squeezes. After a minute his breath falls back into the measured sound of sleep.

Undressing him last night, Pia had asked again, 'Why did you stop being a doctor?' And at last he had answered her. 'I was in a camp.' She wasn't sure what he meant by that, so she said, 'And?' 'And?' he'd repeated, mildly annoyed. He was naked, his body in front of her and his body in profile in the mirror. The room was quiet, except for the hum in her head. 'Well,' he said, 'people died there, for one. A lot of people . . .' And then he looked at his hands.

AT DAWN, THE GROOM IS down on the beach, and this surprises Pia. He's wearing good clothes: a sweater, trousers rolled up to the knees, the wrong footwear. He's moving sluggishly, and Pia intuits that he took the night shift. The beach is still dotted with lanterns. More clothes have washed up, along with parts of the wheelhouse. A dozen life vests have been lined up near the cliff wall.

Pia hands out tea to the silent group; the small talk from the day before is gone. The six on the beach—the barman, the widow's son, Pia, the builder, the groom, and the farmer, whose dog is trotting the tide line—keep their focus on the sea. Pia thinks of the poet her mother loved—the one who wrote about grief: how few of the angels were singing, how few dogs were barking, about shutting a balcony door so as not to hear the sobbing. Here, she thinks, the balcony door is the sea.

IN THE LAST RECORDING Pia's mother made, she enters a house of dissidents in hiding. She describes where she is and what exactly is happening: 'We are being led into the house under escort . . .' '. . . there are ten people huddled in the dark of a kitchen . . .' '. . . there's a sense among those gathered that the government will be overthrown . . .' She does not speak as a citizen whose government might fall; she does not speak as someone who will be detained and tortured under a new regime, under excuses for cruelty. She doesn't see her own death in front of her. She isn't even angry.

Now, Pia stands by the sea, thinking about how she has the ability to move her mother's interviews around in her mind: she can play them back and forth in and out of order, take the flower of history and turn it into a seed. She thinks of the philosopher who wrote about mirrors: *Mirrors can only record what can be seen. They ask for nothing and give back exactly what they receive.* She watches the builder, standing at the tide line with binoculars. After a few minutes, he comes jogging back up the beach. Before he reaches her, she remembers standing in front of the mirror on the landing in the hotel— her mother's face present in her own, and some other form unveiling itself through the hum of the night's wine. She closes her eyes tight and only the sound of the sea remains. She compares the surf rolling and lightly crashing to the way the sea in the village where she grew up poured over and through the pebbles in the bay, dice the sea was shaking.

THE FIRST BODY TO COME IN is a man's. This is followed by a woman's, then a boy's. They come bobbing toward the shore, and the barman and the widow's son drag the adults up from the tide line. The boy is so light he can be lifted in the builder's arms.

The bodies are laid out on the sand. They're veined and bloated, the skin waterlogged and lifted away from the bones. They've come in without clothes so that you can see every violence. It's almost impossible to look: the vulnerability of their nakedness, the gasp of shock on the man's face, the woman's swollen legs, the boy's front teeth, broken.

'Imagine—' the groom says, his eyes welling. And he turns away.

STANDING BESIDE THE SEA'S FROTH, its opaque blue, Pia thinks that the philosopher who wrote about mirrors and glassy surfaces is wrong: this sea has no reflection . . . even the word 'sea' fails. This sea doesn't resemble the sea of the village in the country where she grew up. Even to name a body of water seems insufficient in this instant—an instant where a woman's dark and tangled hair slicks to the side of her face, a face so decimated that the word 'face' is inadequate, too.

The islanders lift the woman's body into one of the heavy black bags. They set her down gently and zip up the front so that she disappears. They do this with the boy, and again with the man. The barman takes his binoculars and goes back to the shore. The builder and the widow's son move up and down the beach, laying out more bags. Soon there is a line of thirty across the sand.

ON HER WAY BACK TO THE HOTEL, Pia passes the widow's house. The widow is standing in her large picture window, her hair set in tidy white curls, her cardigan buttoned up properly. She raises her hand to wave at Pia but her expression remains neutral, as if she isn't sure whether Pia is real or a figment moving through one of her own dissembling dreams.

The desk clerk at the hotel asks Pia what's happening down on the beach, and Pia requests a pad of paper and a pen. She can hear her mother saying, 'and on the third morning . . .' and 'these events come at a time when . . .'

In the bar, the bride and her father silently play a game of cards.

PIA RETURNS TO THE BEACH, again almost slipping down the embankment. She makes it to the skirt of rocks and stops to gather her breath. She's tired now, and her vision is blurry. She touches the bump on her head. Still, she begins to work. She unzips the body bag of the man who came in first. She writes down his exact description: how tall he is, the length of his hair, the shape of his eyes, how his toes are long and almost uniform in length. She touches him every-where—she lifts his arm, rolls him over, and in turning him she feels the heft of him and thinks about how he was once alive and woke up in a bed and rolled his body toward the sun. There is a scar on his hand: a thin line of white skin. She writes this down, draws its likeness. She is trying to write a message to the future, to someone who might need these notes, who might read this description and say, *This was my brother,* or *This was my uncle,* or *This was my friend.*

THE MAN AND THE WOMAN are wearing simple wedding rings. He has one brown shoe tied tightly to his bloated foot. His beard is matted. She is wearing a delicate silver bracelet. The boy has dark hair, and a birthmark on his left calf the size of a thumbprint. Pia draws its location and shape in her book.

Farther down the beach, more locals arrive. They stand on the rocks, waiting. The woman from the grocer's has binoculars, and the fisherman has put on hip waders. He's carrying a hook on a long pole and he walks with it out into the froth. The dog is still doing his work along the tide line, his tongue hanging out the side of his mouth. The builder walks into the waves until he's up to his waist, and then he grabs at something—a grey mass—and wades back to the shore with it.

PIA MAKES HERSELF REMEMBER this: When Pia's mother left her at the fountain in the plaza long ago, when her mother went off with a man who bundled her into his car, when her mother disappeared, Pia managed to find her way home on her own. She got up from under the blearing leaves after hours and hours of waiting and she started to run. She ran and ran, past the pastel faces of the houses and the wrought-iron balconies, the hanging laundry, the white cat with his back arched and the men and women sitting patiently on benches under the drooping trees. She ran as fast as she could, and a part of her knew where she was going even as she felt lost and alone.

THE SUN COMES UP. Pia is standing on the sand, her head heavy with exhaustion. She squints out at the water, says over and over: *Stay awake.* A part of her is here and a part of her sees this catastrophe as if it is far away—as if it's something her mother might have covered, or a report she's glanced at in the morning paper before finishing her coffee and heading out the door. But there's a slop of seaweed next to her feet, and her hands are freezing.

Suddenly, in the distance, people are moving. There's a surge of energy on the beach. Pia's breath hitches and she feels her chest lift in a sudden inhalation. Then stillness. And then again—a gasp and ragged breath.

Out past the harbour, past the twin points of the headland, a ship steams south.

No: Out past the harbour—a rescue boat.

Pia closes her eyes. *Stay here,* she thinks, *stay here.*

She forces her eyes open. The bodies are coming in.

Look.

ACKNOWLEDGEMENTS

This book would not have been possible without the love and support of my late husband, Glenn Hunter. Even as he was dying he encouraged me to keep writing it. In his last weeks he was still helping with factual, historical and worldly knowledge—as he has done with every book I've ever written.

Thanks to Claudia Casper, who saw me through the dark times and who always affirmed the value of literary work. To Kerry Ohana, who keeps me on this earth. To my mother and sister for showing up time and time again. To Helen and Tony, Jill and Derek, Jade and Brigette, Sue, James, Anne, Sam and Jen, Leslie, Carissa, Maureen, Betsy, Tom and Kalissa, Miranda, Sibeal and Peter, Sue and Bruce, and Doug and Liz, who stood with us and witnessed. To my brother, Lee, and Leitha, in the US, and to Rochelle and Pat in St. John's, and Angela in the UK for light and love from a distance. To my former writing students who showed up with grace and kindness and plants. To Glenn's family—Deanna, Laurie and Rob—for the gift of your care and in honour of your grief.

To Joel Thomas Hynes, Anosh Irani and Helen Humphreys for friendship and solidarity in the trenches. To Shaun O'Mara, who graciously stepped up and answered the sorts of technical questions Glenn would have answered, and who gifted me with understanding and love. To Cooper, Juniper and Clara, who sustain me and bring me joy every day.

I'm grateful to the Canada Council for their support of this work, and to Kwantlen Polytechnic University for a research grant that enabled me to spend time in Portbou. The Canadian Forces Artist Program provided me with an invaluable opportunity to think and learn about bearing witness with Canadian and NATO forces during a mission in 2018.

The Dermot Healy epigraph at the start of the book is from his poem 'The Quick Slow Boat' in *The Travels of Sorrow* (The Gallery Press, 2015) reproduced by kind permission of the author's estate c/o The Gallery Press. The Federico García Lorca epigraph is from his poem 'Narcissus.'

I'm full of gratitude for the wonderful team at Knopf Canada and at Penguin Random House, especially Kristin Cochrane, Anne Collins, Rick Meier, Kelly Hill, and Sharon Klein. Thanks to Suzanne Brandreth and the team at Cooke International for championing my work in the world.

While this book is a work of fiction, aspects of it were inspired by the life and death of Walter Benjamin (1892–1940), whose alleged suicide in Portbou, Spain, informed a portion of this fiction's plot. Benjamin was a great thinker and his work and words are a stunning legacy. In 1918, Malcolm MacNeill, a police officer on the island of Islay, filled a journal with descriptions of the dead after a tragic shipwreck. His journals and act of witness also inspired this novel.

Last, thank you to Lynn Henry—a brilliant editor and remarkable friend. Every project we work on together makes me a better thinker, a stronger writer and a more expansive human being. Your compassion during the writing and revising of this novel made the book possible.

AISLINN HUNTER is an award-winning novelist and poet and the author of seven highly acclaimed books including the novel *The World Before Us*, which was a *New York Times* Editor's Choice, a *Guardian* and NPR "Book of the Year," and winner of the Ethel Wilson Fiction Prize. Her work has been adapted into music, dance, art, and film forms—including a feature film based on her novel *Stay*, which premiered at the Toronto International Film Festival. Hunter holds degrees in Creative Writing, Art History, Writing and Cultural Politics, and English Literature. In 2018 she served as a Canadian War Artist working with Canadian and NATO forces. She teaches creative writing and lives in Vancouver, BC.